Covert Exposure
A Nick Spinelli Mystery

Valerie J. Clarizio

Published by
Melange Books, LLC
White Bear Lake, MN 55110
www.melange-books.com

Cover Art by Caroline Andrus

Covert Exposure
Valerie J. Clarizio

Detective Spinelli's life is tossed sideways when he is reassigned from the Homicide division to assist in the Child Services division of the Social Services Department for the holiday season. From the beginning, Spinelli and Caseworker Shannon O'Hara generate their own kind of fireworks, causing more than the normal workplace stress. They both have their own philosophies for dealing with the clientele. However, the forces of nature have their own plan for Spinelli and Shannon.

Shannon moonlights as Santa Claus' little helper at the mall, and when Santa and an elf turn up dead Shannon appears to be next on the killer's list. Spinelli is placed back on homicide and goes undercover as Santa to help capture the killer. He catches a great deal of grief along the way but will he capture the heart of his little Santa's helper as well?

Dedication

To my husband, Rick. Thanks for washing the dishes and entertaining the cat so I could lock myself in the computer room to write.

To my brothers. Thanks for the tidbits of male perspective you provided to me whether I wanted them or not.

A special thank you to my first critique partner, Virginia McCullough, who taught me about the craft of writing, and red-lined my first manuscript more than I care to admit.

Last but not least, thank you Darla Tong for taking the time to read and re-read every manuscript I wrote until I got it right.

Chapter One

Spinelli held his coffee mug high. "Congratulations, partner, you made it through. Enjoy your retirement. Here's to Mad Dog Maxwell."

Shouts of "Congratulations" rippled through the downtown Milwaukee precinct as the detectives toasted Maxwell with their coffee and doughnuts in hand.

Spinelli watched Mad Dog smile and nod at everyone as he carried a cardboard box stuffed with a career's worth of personal belongings out the door for the last time. Everything he knew about being a great homicide detective, he'd learned from that man. He missed him already.

Mad Dog was the only one who gave him the time of day when he started on the force as a snot-nosed hotshot kid some years ago.

"Spinelli," Captain Jackson barked.

His eyes came into focus. "Yeah."

"I need to talk to you," she yelled across the room as she waved him over.

Jackson took a seat behind her desk as he entered her office. "Shut the door, Spinelli."

He did as she asked, then fixed his gaze on her. He stepped back and rested his butt on the two-drawer file cabinet next to her desk.

"What's up, Cap?" he asked as he raked his hand through his hair.

"You've been temporarily assigned to Social Services and you will need to report to Ms. Fontaine on the fourth floor until further notice."

A chuckle escaped Spinelli's lips. He turned his head to glance through Jackson's office windows toward the detective desks located

1

immediately outside her office doors. He looked for the mastermind behind the practical joke but he saw none. Not one detective in the office looked in his direction as he hoped they would as they waited for the joke to take hold. He cut his eyes back to the Captain. "This is a joke, right?"

She shook her head. "This is no joke, Detective. Until further notice, you've been assigned to Social Services. The holiday season is tough on that department and they need extra hands with child recovery and placement."

Spinelli sprang to his feet and stepped toward her desk. "Captain, you're shitting me, right? Child recovery and placement. What the hell is that crap?"

Spinelli reached toward his chest, lifted the gold colored badge hanging by a chain around his neck, and centered it directly in front of Jackson's eyes. "In case you don't remember, this is a detective badge. I'm a homicide detective, not a child recovery and placement detective."

Jackson rose to her feet and pointed at the white lettering on the glass of her office door, which simply read *Captain Jackson*. "In case you don't remember Detective, I'm Captain Jackson. You've been reassigned to Social Services until further notice. Ms. Fontaine is waiting for you upstairs."

Spinelli stared at the Captain for a moment, his mind racing for a reasonable excuse as to why he shouldn't be reassigned. "But my clearance record, it's impeccable. Shouldn't that mean something? And we're short staffed down here as it is."

Jackson shifted her eyes away from Spinelli, looking past him and through the glass windows of her office. She pointed toward his crime board. "That's just it, Spinelli. Your board's almost clean and the other teams are overloaded with open cases. As for staff shortages, with the Mayor's budget cuts and directive to not replace retiring staff every department is short staffed. Additionally, you're the only Detective right now without a partner. You're the logical choice to be transferred."

"But…"

Jackson raised her hand, cutting him off. "No buts, you're it. And you can still help out down here when you're not needed upstairs."

Air hissed from his lungs, drowning out the words she spoke.

2

Spinelli lifted his gaze to meet hers; the look in her eyes told him the deal was done. He fought hard to find a voice, "How long? How long must I do this?"

"Again, it's a temporary assignment just for the holidays. The holidays are tough on the Social Services department. Their clientele…well, it's a tough time of year for everyone, those folks especially."

Chapter Two

Spinelli willed his right foot to step forward, then his left foot. "Repeat motion," he whispered to himself until he reached the stairwell. He chose not to take the elevator. That would be too quick. He needed time to let his new assignment sink in. His mind spun to find ways to get out of it. Within minutes, he found himself standing in front of a glass paneled door with the words "Department of Social Services" etched in the glass. His long legs carried him up the stairs faster than he desired.

He sucked in a deep breath, lifted his hand, and pushed the door open. He stepped through the doorway and into the reception area where he paused to take a look around. A cold chill ran up his spine as he studied the packed area. He noted that the clientele consisted of mostly women and children. He watched the children for a moment as they noisily played about the room. His ears registered a decibel level of at least two-hundred plus, far louder than any dirt-track stockcar race he'd ever attended. He lifted his fingers to his temples and pressed slightly but the throbbing continued.

With his eyes still focused on the children, he took a step toward the reception desk and accidently caught his foot inside a dollhouse. He tumbled forward, his heart racing, his breath quickening, and his hands uselessly flailing. He took a header right smack dab into the front of the receptionist's desk and darkness fell upon him.

Spinelli opened his eyes to find several children gazing down at him. He bounced up as quickly as a weeble wobble and rapidly looked about the room but the second he planted himself on his feet the room started to spin. He felt a small set of hands firmly gripping his left arm just above his elbow. A warm sensation flowed through his arm and into his core. He placed the palm of his right hand on the receptionist's desk and leaned on it for support.

"Are you going to be okay?" a soft feminine voice sang throughout his head.

The sweet sound trailed off and silence filled the air.

The voice sang through his head again. "Are you okay? Do you need to sit down?"

Spinelli willed his eyes in the direction of the voice. He squeezed them shut, swallowed hard, and opened them again. Shades of emerald green danced before him. He blinked quickly several times, each blink bringing him closer to heaven. He thought for sure the eyes of an angel were on him and the pearly gates stood behind her.

He cleared his throat and found his voice. "I'm fine. I'm Detective Spinelli, I'm here to see Ms. Fontaine. She should be expecting me."

The woman with the emerald green angel-eyes released her grip from his arm but the warmth of her touch remained. She motioned for him to follow her. Spinelli followed "Angel-Eyes" down a long narrow corridor. He studied the back of her starting with the shiny bright red hair-bun stationed high on the back of her head. Not one hair was out of place. He lowered his eyes to her inviting soft-looking milky white neck and continued on to her petite shoulders. The navy blue blazer draped over them perfectly matched the navy blue skirt she wore. The length of her skirt fell just above her knees allowing him to take in the sight of her thin yet shapely legs. He shifted his eyes up and down several times, memorizing the backside of the woman whose soft feminine voice still sang in his head. He concluded that her conservative navy suit and "old lady" hair-bun did not match the intense sexiness of her bright green eyes.

His body swayed forward, then back, as he halted on a dime, nearly bumping into his green-eyed angel when she stopped in the doorway of Ms. Fontaine's office.

"Ms. Fontaine, Detective Spinelli is here to see you," the woman said as she stepped inside the office and gestured for him to follow.

Spinelli studied the large woman with graying hair who sat behind the desk. She removed her wire-rimmed reading glasses and let them fall onto her chest pulling the colorful beaded chain taut. She rose to her feet and extended her hand toward him. He shook her hand.

Ms. Fontaine pointed toward the chairs opposite her desk. "Please, Detective, take a seat."

"Shannon, you may as well take a seat and get acquainted with Detective Spinelli since he is who you will be working with."

Ms. O'Hara. She's the case worker you are assigned to."

Spinelli watched as "Angel Eyes" took a seat in the chair next to him. She crossed her legs causing her skirt to rise up her thigh. His eyes fixed on her shapely thigh. She quickly reached over her leg and tugged her skirt toward her knee covering as much of her leg as the material would allow.

His heart picked up pace at the thought of working with this beautiful green-eyed creature for the next several weeks. He glanced at her and accepted his reward from God for being forced to leave the homicide division.

Spinelli listened as Ms. Fontaine explained his role for the next several weeks. Basically, he would aid Ms. O'Hara with child recovery and placement, and whatever else she needed assistance with. Ms. Fontaine told him how much their clientele struggle with the holiday season. She further stated that the holiday season proved to be a season high in domestic abuse, which resulted in large numbers of children having to be removed from their homes and placed in foster care.

Spinelli nodded at Ms. Fontaine, accepting his role, though still wondering how long this banishment would last.

Chapter Three

Spinelli followed Shannon to her office, unable to peel his eyes from her shapely legs. His nostrils narrowed, sucking in every ounce of the sweet scent that lingered in the air behind her. She gestured for him to take a seat in a chair opposite her desk. Her phone rang and she picked up the receiver as she sat down. As she spoke on the telephone, he scanned her small office memorizing every detail like detectives tend to do. He couldn't help but notice how just a touch of feminine warmth accented the professional décor. His eyes shifted from the photo of an older couple, perhaps in their early seventies, to a photo of three little red-headed boys. He wondered if the boys belonged to her. He glanced at her left hand, no ring.

Shannon hung up the phone receiver. "I'm sorry about that, Detective Spinelli," she said as she thumbed through the mounds of neatly organized stacks of case files on her desk, "here it is…the Washington file."

Spinelli watched as she flipped the file open and lost herself in the information for a brief moment. She blew out a sigh and looked up at him. He could easily see the sadness flood her big green eyes. Shannon cleared her throat. "The authorities picked up Gilbert Washington early this morning as a result of a domestic abuse call."

"What happened? What did he do?" he asked as he leaned back in his chair and crossed his arms over his chest.

"Apparently the neighbor placed the 911 call when he heard Gilbert and his wife, Charmane, arguing. A loud thud followed the arguing. The neighbor assumed the cause of the thud was Gilbert throwing Charmane against the wall. As it turned out the neighbor was right. Unfortunately the kids witnessed the entire exchange."

Shannon shook her head. "We've offered Charmane assistance for herself and her children but she refuses to leave Gilbert. As a result, today we will be removing the children from the home and placing them in foster care."

"Why does she refuse to leave him?"

"Scared perhaps." Shannon sighed and shook her head. "And he's probably her crack supplier."

"Is Gilbert still in lockup?"

"Yes, so it would probably be a good idea to head over there and remove the children before he's released."

"I'll get my unmarked and meet you up front," Spinelli replied as he sprang to his feet and headed for the door. Before his third step hit the floor he heard Shannon call his name. He turned to find her standing behind her desk holding up a set of keys.

He cocked his head to the side. "What?"

"We'll take one of the vehicles assigned to Social Services. They're fully equipped with car seats for matters such as these," Shannon said as she handed the keys to him. "You can drive so I can review the file some more."

"Car seats? How many children are we talking about here?"

"Three. The oldest, Lesha is seven, Darius is three and Christina is nine months old."

Spinelli followed Shannon to the parking lot. She pointed at a dark green Dodge minivan. "That's the one."

He shifted his eyes from the minivan to Shannon and then back to the van. "That, we're taking that?" No red lights, no sirens, no excitement. Life as he knew it was slipping away from him.

"Perhaps you could just get in and drive, and forget the comments," Shannon said as she climbed in through the passenger door.

Spinelli got in on the driver's side and started the engine. He adjusted the seat to accommodate his long legs, then the mirrors. Once he finished altering everything, he glanced over at Shannon.

"What?" she asked.

He shook his head. "I'm just wondering how I got here. Yesterday I was a homicide detective and today I'm driving a minivan that smells like sweaty socks."

"I'm sorry you're not pleased with your assignment but we need to get going if we are going to remove the children before Gilbert makes bail."

Spinelli put the minivan in drive and headed toward the Washington home located just north of downtown, on Cherry Street. He knew that area could mean trouble. His senses moved into "full alert" mode.

As he drove, Shannon explained the procedure for removing the children. She would do all the talking and he would stand in the background as an authority figure to help keep peace during the process.

Spinelli parked in front of the Washington's apartment building. Shannon reached for the door handle but immediately halted when Spinelli wrapped his hand around the upper part of her left arm. "Wait a second," he said as he scanned the area.

The neighborhood left a lot to be desired. The old multi-story apartment buildings screamed for repair. The most up-to-date gang signs cluttered the apartment's exterior and clusters of homeless people paraded about the sidewalk picking through the litter sprawled about the area as they pushed their belongings in wheeled carts. At least on this particular day the sunlight lit up the street making it easy for Spinelli to see and assess his surroundings. Just the opposite of the last time he visited this neighborhood when darkness filled the street making it difficult to find his enemies. In fact, if it weren't for the stench of death penetrating the night air he may never have located and apprehended Magoo and Slapshot, two hoods responsible for the deaths of four members of their rival gang.

When Spinelli deemed the area secure, he gave Shannon the okay to exit the minivan. He caught a glimpse of her eye roll. "Hey, I'm just making sure it's secure for your own good," he growled.

Spinelli followed Shannon into the apartment building and up three flights of rickety stairs, gripping the handrail more firmly with each passing step. Stale dry air swept through the narrow corridor, stinging his lungs with each breath he took. The floor felt spongy under his feet and the hallway lights cut in and out, as they pleased. The intense aroma of decaying mice made his eyes water. He absently patted them with the sleeve of his jacket.

Shannon knocked on the Washington's apartment door. A young girl answered. Spinelli studied her. He figured she must be Lesha, the oldest of the children.

"Mama, Ms. O'Hara's here," Lesha yelled over her shoulder.

"No school today?" Shannon asked as she stepped through the doorway.

"Daddy told Mama that we couldn't go anywhere until he gets back," Lesha innocently replied.

Charmane rounded the corner from the hallway and stepped into the living room. When she glanced toward Shannon, she started to smile until she noticed Spinelli standing in the doorway. Charmane threw her hand over her heart and the black and blue eyes she sported immediately swelled with tears.

Well, I guess she knows why we're here...Christ, Spinelli thought.

As Shannon explained the process to Charmane, Spinelli scanned the small filthy apartment. Mildew lined the tan colored fabric on the couch where Lesha sat and watched television. Dirty dishes and soda cans covered the end tables, and dirt-smudged toys littered the floor. The bubbling wallpaper reeked of dampness, a piece of plywood covered one of the two windows in the living room, and the entryway closet door hung crooked by only one hinge. The apartment wasn't fit for a litter of feral cats.

Charmane began to sob hysterically and begged Shannon not to take her children. Spinelli shifted his eyes to Lesha and watched her as she continued to stare at the television, not once looking in her hysterical mother's direction. He noted how Darius, on the other hand, clung to his mother's leg and sobbed along with her. He wondered if three-year-old Darius even understood why his mother cried. And if that wasn't enough, the screams of baby Christina began to bellow from down the hall. Charmane shook Darius from her leg, and headed down the hall. She returned moments later with Christina in her arms and Darius resumed his leg-clinging position. She continued to beg Shannon not to take the children.

Spinelli watched as Shannon turned her attention from Charmane to

Lesha and held her hand out toward her. "Lesha, honey, it's time for us to go."

Lesha simply rose from the couch and took Shannon's hand. Shannon held her other hand out to Darius but he refused to let go of his mother's leg. "Come on, Sweetie, we need to go now," Shannon said softly. Darius still refused.

This production went on for what seemed like an eternity to Spinelli, and he knew for sure that the noise level produced by Charmane, Darius, and the baby would permanently deafen him if he didn't remedy the situation immediately. He walked over to Charmane and simply plucked the screaming baby out of her arms and plunked her into Shannon's free arm, then he reached down and broke Darius' grip on his mother's leg, lifted him up and perched him on his hip, and then motioned for Shannon to follow him. Charmane dropped to her knees threw her hands over her face and wept into them.

Spinelli turned on his heel and refused to look back. On his way out of the apartment he stopped by the hall closet and retrieved three small jackets looking close to the sizes needed and he exited the apartment.

Spinelli followed Shannon out of the building. When they reached the minivan, she loaded the kids in and took her place in the passenger seat. She spoke not a word.

Darius and Christina continued their wailing as Spinelli drove to the address of the foster home. He watched and listened to Shannon as she interacted with the children. He couldn't help but notice how her soft soothing voice and warm eyes calmed them.

Spinelli helped carry the kids into the foster home and then went back to the minivan and waited for Shannon to complete her business. He leaned his head back against the headrest. He found himself daydreaming about his good old life as a homicide detective. Only hours passed since he last worked on a homicide case but at this very moment, it felt like decades to him.

Spinelli snapped out of his daydream when Shannon opened the door and slid into the passenger seat.

"Where to now? What's next on our agenda?" he asked as he signaled and pulled away from the curb.

Out of the corner of his eye, he saw Shannon suck her plump ruby red bottom lip into her mouth and chew on it for a moment. She released her lip and sucked in a deep breath. "Back to the office. Just take me back to the office."

The coolness in her voice sent a shiver throughout Spinelli's body. Half an hour ago, this woman's voice seemed so soft and soothing but now it seemed cold and hard as ice.

Spinelli stopped at a red light and turned his head in her direction. "Well how does this work? We do this type of thing all day or what?"

Spinelli observed her face. Sometime in the last hour or so, it transitioned from its soft smooth looking milky white color to the reddest of all reds. The heat escaping her pores warmed the entire vehicle without the help of the van's heater. Spinelli unzipped his jacket. Shannon sat silent, staring forward. "What, what the hell's the matter?" he asked.

She slowly turned in his direction and when her eyes met his he felt as though they grabbed a hold of his and clamped on like a vice grip. He fought to break free from her stare but she wouldn't release him. He admired her strength yet it scared the hell out of him. A car horn sounded behind them and he tore his gaze from her and focused it on the green traffic light. He pressed the accelerator toward the floor.

Spinelli parked the minivan in the parking lot. Shannon sprang out of the van like a jack-in-the-box on speed. In two long quick steps, he caught up to her. He reached forward, wrapped his hand around her wrist, and tugged slightly to slow her down. She stopped and spun on her heel to face him. She looked up at him and just stared for a moment, then shook her wrist loose from his grip, spun around and headed into the building.

He stayed on her heels as she nearly sprinted up four flights of stairs.

"Ms. O'Hara," Spinelli called, his voice so high-pitched his own ears hardly recognized it.

Shannon stopped dead in her tracks and turned to face him. She pulled her eyebrows together, and fixed her green eyes on him. He struggled for a voice. Moments passed before he finally asked, "What's wrong? What did I do to piss you off so much?"

Shannon took a step toward him, raised her hand, and pointed her petite pale finger in his face. She clenched her teeth and then spoke through them. "You, I have never encountered such coldness from another human being in my entire life. Do you have any idea what you put that family through, ripping the children from their mother's arms like that?"

Spinelli watched as her body shuddered. He cocked his head to the side and pulled a frown. "Let me get this right, you're pissed at me because I yanked a couple of screaming kids out the arms of a crack whore. Aren't you the reason we showed up on her doorstep in the first place? Wasn't it your call to remove the kids from the home? The way I see it you should be thanking me for getting your job done for you."

"Thanking you, I should be thanking you? Are you nuts? Those kids were devastated. There is a protocol to handling this type of situation, which you totally shot out the window. I can't believe they sent someone like you to work in our department," Shannon bit back.

His blood boiled. "What do you mean someone like me? You mean someone who'll tell these crack whores and child abusers that we're not going to put up with their crap? It's because of people like you, and your touchy feely bullshit, that these pieces of shit keep living the way they do and treating their kids the way they do."

Spinelli watched as Shannon closed her eyes and drew in a couple of deep breaths. He reached toward her. She raised her hand and held it inches from his chest. She shook her head. "I can't talk to you right now or I'll just say things, things that aren't nice."

Shannon turned, pushed her way through the stairwell doorway, and walked down the hall toward her office. Spinelli stared after her.

Spinelli took two steps back and leaned against the wall of the stairwell. He crossed his arms over his chest and stared down at his feet. Sweat began to bead on his brow and his vision blurred as horrible memories of his past surfaced. To make matters worse the harsh words Shannon spoke seconds earlier rotated through his mind over and over with the unpleasant memories. *I can't believe they sent someone like you to work in our department. I can't believe they sent someone like you to work in our department. I can't believe they sent someone like you to work in our department.* He wondered what exactly she meant. She knew nothing about him or his life. He squeezed his eyes shut hoping to extinguish the awful childhood memories. It didn't work. *Cherry Street, of all places why did the Washington home have to be on Cherry Street?* The very same street where he grew up.

Spinelli opened his eyes and absently glanced around the stairwell. He wasn't quite sure what to do with himself now. Should he go back downstairs to his precinct or should he go back up to Social Services? He chose to head downstairs to his precinct, to his comfortable life.

Chapter Four

Spinelli stepped through the doorway of his precinct to find Walker and Marsh gathered around their open-case board. He stood behind them taking in their conversation and he watched as Walker hung photos of a dead body on the board.

Spinelli leaned forward and studied the photos. "You gotta be kidding me. Is that Santa Claus?"

Walker turned to face Spinelli. "Sure is. He took a 22 round to the back of his head. The medical examiner put the time of death at about 11:00 last night, about two hours after the mall closed."

Spinelli crossed his arms over his chest as he continued to study the photos. "What do we know?"

"Motive looks like robbery. His wallet's missing. Mall security identified him as Roland Hudson, age sixty-eight. They said he's been playing Santa at the mall for years," Marsh added.

Spinelli was about to ask more questions when he heard the shrill voice of Captain Jackson yelling his name. He squeezed his eyes shut and wished himself anywhere but in the office at that very moment.

"Yeah Cap. What's up?" he asked in his smooth self-assured voice.

"In my office now!" she demanded.

Spinelli exchanged glances with Walker and Marsh and headed toward his death sentence. The second he entered the Captain's office she met his gaze. She hadn't said a word but he felt like he'd been scolded and beat to a pulp. He took a seat in the chair opposite her desk and watched her large nostrils flare in and out. Jackson ran her hand through her thick short black hair and cleared her throat. "What did you do to Ms. O'Hara? You've been upstairs less than half a day and her boss is already calling down here looking for a replacement for you. Fontaine said she's never seen O'Hara so upset."

Jackson leaned forward and placed her elbows on her desk, resting her chin on her fingers as she stared down her nose at Spinelli. Though she only stood about five-foot-five and weighed all of one hundred thirty pounds, she managed to scare the hell out of him at times. He shifted his body in the chair leaning back to make himself more comfortable. "I don't know. I just helped her take a few kids out of a crack whore's home. I guess maybe she didn't like how I did it."

Spinelli flashed his lady-killer smile at Jackson to try to loosen her up a bit but it didn't work. "Spinelli, I don't have time for this crap. Why can't you ever just play nice with people?"

He opened his mouth to speak but Jackson cut him off. "I told Fontaine that you are all that is available right now and she'll just need to make due. I told her I would talk to you and that you would do whatever she and Ms. O'Hara instructed you to do. Have I made myself clear, Detective?"

"Yes, ma'am."

"Now get your ass back out there and work with Walker and Marsh on the Santa Claus case until Ms. O'Hara needs you. You're going to give her the rest of the afternoon to simmer down. She doesn't need your services again until tomorrow. And Spinelli, try to soften up a bit."

He fought to not roll his eyes as he lifted himself from his chair. Well, on a good note at least he got to work on something productive for the remainder of the afternoon.

Chapter Five

Spinelli arrived at the precinct bright and early Friday morning in hopes to study Walker and Marsh's Santa board before reporting to Ms. O'Hara.

He nudged his way between Walker and Marsh. "Anything new on Santa?"

"His blood alcohol level came back at .06. No sign of struggle. Just the .22 to the back of the head," Walker replied as he flipped open the manila folder and scanned the medical examiner's report. Spinelli leaned toward him and craned his neck to review the report as well.

Spinelli finished reading the report and took a couple of steps toward the Santa board then he looked back at Walker and Marsh. "So he played Santa until 9:00 p.m., the Coroner put his time of death at about 11:00 p.m., his blood alcohol level came back at .06, and they found him in the mall's parking ramp a few stalls away from his vehicle. So he drank alcohol at the mall? Any reason he would still be at the mall two hours after his shift ended? And where, when and with who did he drink?"

Walker closed the folder then tossed it onto his cluttered desk. "Marsh and I questioned the security guards that were on duty between 9:00 p.m. and the time he was found and nobody seems to know anything. We're going back over to the mall again today to review more security tapes and talk to more mall employees."

Spinelli noted the time. He raked his hand through his hair and willed his feet to move in the direction of the stairwell leading to the

17

fourth floor.

Within minutes, he found himself knocking on Ms. O'Hara's office door. Before she could even look up from her desk, he strapped on his lady-killer smile hoping it would smooth things over. "Good morning, Ms. O'Hara. Reporting for duty."

Shannon looked up from her desk and spoke through her clenched jaw. "Morning, Detective Spinelli."

Spinelli kept his gaze fixed on her. She looked angry and she looked as though she wanted to say more but he wasn't sure he wanted her to. He cleared his throat to speak, to take control of the moment, but she beat him to it.

"Well Detective Spinelli, Ms. Fontaine tells me we're stuck with each other. And just for the record, I'm well aware of the fact you don't want to be here and I'm sure you are aware of the fact that I don't want you here, but I promised Ms. Fontaine that I would do my best to work with you for the next several weeks. So how about we start fresh today and put yesterday behind us?"

Spinelli thought for a moment. He knew he didn't have a choice in the matter. Jackson would string him up if he screwed up again. Oh how he missed Mad Dog. *This is all Mad Dog's fault. If he hadn't retired I wouldn't be in this predicament.* Spinelli offered a crooked smile and nodded. "Okay, fresh start it is."

"Great then, and just so we're clear, your behavior yesterday in the Washington home was completely out of line. And in order for this arrangement to work we need to just stick to the plan which basically means that you need to keep quiet and do as you're told," Shannon replied, unable to hide the disdain in her tone.

Ouch.

Spinelli opened his mouth to defend himself but thought better of it when an image of Captain Jackson's unpleasant glare flashed through his mind. He pressed his lips together.

Spinelli stepped into Shannon's office and took a seat in the chair opposite her desk. He leaned back in the chair and stretched out his legs, making himself at home. He stared across the desk at her and wondered if she wore her hair in that "old lady" bun every day or if perhaps, she let it down at times. The dull suit she wore today reminded him of the drab suit she wore yesterday but rather than navy blue today's version came in a frumpy dark brown color. He wondered if she ever wore clothes that suited her age and petite, yet shapely, body. He imagined she might look pretty hot in one of those fitted sweater dresses gathered tightly at her waist with a big clunky belt. He further imagined her in a pair of sexy tall black boots.

He looked on as Shannon dug through the neatly stacked files on her desk. "Here it is. The Smith file," she said as she flipped the file open and drummed her fingers on her desk as she scanned the contents.

Spinelli fought the urge to reach over and place his hand over her drumming fingers.

Shannon closed the file and looked up at him. "We need to do an unannounced visit today at the home of Mike and Tiffany Smith."

"What's the story?" Spinelli asked.

"The Smiths...well they're a little...shall we say slow. They're trying to care for a three month old but it's not going very well."

"What part isn't going well?"

Shannon sucked in a deep breath then exhaled. "Well, the Smiths are in their mid-thirties but their academic level is somewhere in the neighborhood of about the fifth grade level. They've made numerous visits to the emergency room with the baby."

Spinelli frowned and quickly shifted his body forward toward Shannon's desk. "Why? What did they do to the baby?"

"Nothing, they haven't really done anything to the baby. They just don't know how to care for her. They don't even know the basics. The baby cries and they don't know what to do so they take her to the emergency room."

Spinelli flashed an accusing scowl in Shannon's direction. "Well if they don't know how to care for a baby why is the baby still in their custody? I guess this is our great system at work, huh."

"Well, I'm sorry you don't like our system, Detective, but it's just not all that simple sometimes. Rather than debate this maybe we should just get a move on, and maybe today you can just stick to your part of the job and let me do mine. Shall we?" Shannon added as she flung her double-breasted wool coat over her shoulders, and motioned for him to leave her office.

Spinelli followed Shannon to the parking lot where they climbed into the same green minivan they had used the day before. He drove them to the Smith home, which happened to be only a few blocks from the Washington home. He parked the vehicle and scanned the area looking for anything unusual or unsafe.

Spinelli hated this neighborhood, the neighborhood in which he grew up, the same neighborhood in which his mother sold herself on the street corner for money to buy crack. He recalled the many times she left him home alone to fend for himself for as long as he could remember until finally, at the ripe old age of thirty-two, she succeeded in killing herself by drug overdose, leaving him completely on his own at the young age of sixteen. After a couple of years pool hustling and card sharking for a living, he figured out what he should do with his life. He decided that if it was the last thing he ever did he was going to clean up the streets of Milwaukee and make sure no children would ever have to grow up in the same environment he had. He put himself through college and took a job with the Milwaukee Police Department. Tears of rage burned behind his eyes but he wouldn't let them fall. He hadn't cried since he was six years old and he wasn't about to start now.

Spinelli turned toward Shannon and nodded. She opened the passenger door and stepped out of the van.

Shannon led the way through the decrepit old apartment building stained with grit and mold. She stopped in front of apartment 4C but didn't knock right away. She stood at the door for a moment and just listened. Spinelli could hear the faint cries of an infant. Shannon knocked on the door but no one answered. After a brief moment she knocked on the door again and again no one answered. She turned the knob and when the door opened, she stepped through and called, "Tiffany?" No one responded. The cries of the infant continued.

Spinelli followed Shannon as she walked through the living room, then the kitchen and into the hallway leading to the two tiny bedrooms. He pushed aside the stacks of what appeared to be bagged clothing in order to make a wider pathway through the cluttered hallway. He couldn't believe that people lived in such filth.

They entered the baby's room where the baby lay crying in her crib. Shannon reached for the baby and scooped her up into her arms. Spinelli watched as Shannon glanced around the room looking as if searching for something specific. "What are you looking for?" he asked.

"She's soaked through. I need a diaper and change of clothes. And I'd like to know where her parents are."

Spinelli's nose crinkled up. "Oh."

Shannon set the baby back into the crib and started undressing her as Spinelli retrieved a diaper and located a dry sleeper. Once Shannon got the baby cleaned up and in dry clothes, a blanket of silence fell over the apartment but only for a brief moment.

"What is that? Can you hear it?" Spinelli asked as he turned his head in the direction of the closet.

Shannon looked toward the closet as well. Spinelli stepped closer to the closet and just listened for a moment. He looked back at Shannon. "Someone's in there and crying."

Spinelli opened the closet door to find Tiffany sitting on the floor, with her knees pulled to her chest and her arms wrapped tightly around her legs. She rocked back and forth as she whimpered. Tears rolled down her plump rosy cheeks like a faucet fully open. He glanced back at Shannon. "Christ, I think she's having a nervous breakdown."

Shannon stepped around Spinelli to get a better look at Tiffany.

"Tiffany, are you okay?" Shannon asked but Tiffany did not respond.

Shannon handed the baby off to Spinelli giving him no choice but to take her. The second the baby hit his hands his entire body tensed up. He'd never held a baby before. He tried to position her in his arms the same way Shannon did moments earlier but it felt uncomfortable for him. Once he thought everything seemed under control he looked down at the baby's face to find it scrunching up like a large plump raisin then all at once the corners of her little mouth began turning downward. "Uhm, Shannon…Shannon."

"What?" Shannon snapped without looking back at him.

"I think she's going to cry," and before he could get the last syllable out of his mouth the baby began to wail again.

"You need to deal with her Spinelli. There's a bigger issue for me to deal with over here," Shannon replied as she knelt down in front of Tiffany. "Tiffany, what's wrong? What's the matter?" she asked as she slowly reached toward the troubled woman.

The second Shannon's hand touched Tiffany's shoulder Tiffany snapped out of her trance and lunged toward her. She tackled Shannon to the floor and struck her several times before Spinelli grabbed Tiffany by the back of her shirt and pulled her off Shannon.

Tiffany attempted to make a run for it but Spinelli held her shirt too tight and she couldn't free herself. Tiffany spun on her heel to face him, both arms flailing. He shifted his body to protect the baby from the blows. He took a blow to his jaw and shoulder before pushing Tiffany away and face first into the wall. With the baby in one arm and Tiffany secured with the other, Spinelli looked down at Shannon who lay still on the floor. A thin trail of blood led from the corner of her mouth down the side of her chin. She stared wide-eyed at the ceiling.

Spinelli opened and closed his mouth a couple of times to loosen his jaw. "Shannon, are you okay?"

Still looking a little dazed, Shannon glanced about the room. "Yeah, I guess."

"You need to get up and take the baby so I can deal with Miss Tiffany here."

"Okay."

Spinelli continued to hold Tiffany firmly to the wall. She appeared to be running out of steam. She placed the palms of her hands flat against the wall and gave one last push to free herself but Spinelli's strength overpowered her.

Spinelli watched Shannon as he waited for her to pull herself together and get up off the floor. All at once, Spinelli felt a blunt forceful blow to his right side which sent him tumbling toward the floor. He released his grip on Tiffany and shifted in an attempt to shield the baby, but in doing so he landed on top of Shannon causing her to take the full brunt of the fall. He knocked the wind right out of her. He watched as her eyes rolled back into her head and the blood drained from her already pale cheeks. She gasped for air. She appeared unable to fill her lungs. She gasped again.

Spinelli released his hold on the baby letting her rest on the floor and he pushed himself up on all fours. But before he could get up completely someone jumped onto his back and gripped him in a chokehold. He pushed himself into a kneeling position and he used both his arms to reach over his shoulder and grab his assailant around his neck. He pulled the attacker over his shoulder breaking the chokehold then he scrambled to position himself over his assailant, pinning him to the floor.

"Who the hell are you?" Spinelli asked the small man pinned beneath him.

The man fought to release himself but his strength didn't compare to Spinelli's.

"Who the hell are *you* and why were your hands on my wife?" the man spat back.

"I'm Detective Spinelli and your wife assaulted Ms. O'Hara over there."

Still pinning Smith to the floor, Spinelli looked around the room to find the baby lying on the floor crying. He knew she wasn't physically hurt, perhaps just scared. Tiffany sat on the floor with her knees pulled to her chest and her arms wrapped around her legs; she continued to bawl. And poor Shannon fought for air gasp after gasp.

"Shannon, are you okay?"

"Yeah, I guess."

Shannon lifted herself off the floor and walked over to the baby. She picked up the infant, cradled her in her arms, and rocked her back and forth in an attempt to calm her.

Spinelli handcuffed Smith, pulled him to his feet, and stood him next to the wall. "Don't move," he commanded with the authority of a general.

Spinelli pulled out his cell phone and called for an ambulance for Tiffany. By the way she acted, he certainly thought she would be headed for the mental health facility.

Smith heard Spinelli's call for an ambulance. "She doesn't need an ambulance. She needs to stay here and take care of the baby!" he screamed at the top of his lungs.

Before Shannon could explain the situation Spinelli turned in Smith's direction and let loose his anger and frustration. "You're kidding, right?"

Spinelli moved closer to Smith and looked down at him. "Look at her," he yelled as he pointed to Tiffany who continued to sit on the floor in some sort of trance. "Does she look like she's capable of taking care of an infant in that state? She's going to the hospital and that baby is leaving with us."

"Detective, stop!" Shannon yelled drawing Spinelli's attention away from Smith.

He turned to find Shannon staring wide-eyed in his direction, scowling, nostrils flaring, and her cheeks as red as a vine-ripened tomato. The smoke billowing from her ears caused his vision to blur.

She spoke through gritted teeth, "Just stop talking. Let me handle this. Why don't you wait in the hall?"

Spinelli recalled Captain Jackson's words. *Just do as you're told.* Then he sucked in a deep breath. "Fine, handle it then."

Leaving Leaving Shannon unguarded in the bedroom made Spinelli feel uneasy, but he did find a smidgeon of comfort in knowing Smith was handcuffed. However, with as angry as Smith seemed, who knew what he would be capable of, or do, at the height of his irrational fury.

From in the hallway Spinelli could hear Shannon explaining that the baby would be placed in foster care until further notice. He heard her explain the process and what would be required of the Smiths in the event they wanted to see the baby until the court system sorted out the matter.

The baby stopped crying but Spinelli could still hear the whimpers coming from Tiffany. Suddenly he heard Smith scream at Tiffany. "You stupid bitch! You stupid bitch! They're going to take our baby away because you're too dumb to know how to take care of her!"

Spinelli heard the sound of rushing footsteps. He quickly stepped around the doorway and into the baby's room to find Smith kicking at Tiffany who remained seated on the floor. Smith got a couple of hard kicks off before Spinelli grabbed him and pulled him away from his wife. She never even flinched. She just kept rocking herself back and forth.

Moments later, the squad car and ambulance arrived. Two officers hauled Smith away, with Smith kicking and screaming, and the EMTs loaded Tiffany into the ambulance.

Spinelli drove Shannon and the Smith baby to the foster home. The silence in the minivan about killed him and the tension in the air felt thicker than that of a bowl of pea soup, the kind so thick you eat it with a fork.

Spinelli waited in the van while Shannon took care of business in the foster home. He dreaded her return almost as much as he dreaded returning to the office to face Captain Jackson.

He leaned his head back against the headrest, closed his eyes, and replayed the events that occurred in the Smith home. *Damn it, why couldn't I just keep my big mouth shut.* His mind replayed the events again. *Why couldn't I keep my big mouth shut? Because that baby deserves better, that's why!*

Shannon slid into the minivan and slammed the door shut. Her body emitted so much heat Spinelli began to sweat profusely. Her silence about killed him. "Are you going to say anything?" he asked as he continued to drive back to the office.

Spinelli glanced at Shannon and waited for a response. She sat silent. He watched her out of the corner of his eye as she leaned her head back on the headrest, closed her eyes, and drew in slow deep breaths. He gave himself about thirty mental head slaps for being such an idiot. His mind raced for a resolution. Though Shannon had tongue-lashed him earlier in the day, for some reason he just couldn't stand that fact that the beautiful creature who sat beside him disliked him so much. And he couldn't help but think that if only she knew he meant well and was only thinking of the baby's well-being, she wouldn't hate him. In fact, she actually might like him.

Spinelli parked the vehicle and Shannon sprang out and headed toward the building, still without speaking a word. He followed close on her heels. "Come on, Shannon, what did you want me to do? Let him keep wailing on me or you or Tiffany? Do you really want him to go on believing that he and Tiffany are fit for raising children?"

Spinelli's words caused Shannon to stop dead in her tracks. She spun to face him. The rage in her eyes scared the hell out of him. He hunts down killers for a living and none of them ever caused this much fear to penetrate his body.

"Who are you to judge them? Who are you to tell them they aren't fit to be parents? I explained their mental capacity to you so you would know what we were dealing with. All you did was upset them and make things worse."

"You think I made it worse? The way I see it I did them a favor. I'm probably the only person in the world who ever told them the truth. You and I both know that Tiffany doesn't have the ability to raise a child. Why kid them? Why let them believe they can do something they can't?" Spinelli yelled back.

"You know what, Detective Spinelli. When you earn a degree in psychology you can come back and offer me all the free advice you want but until then why don't you just shut the hell up? You know nothing about this. I deal with this day in and day out!"

"O'Hara, you don't know shit about me or what I know. So maybe it's you who should shut the hell up," Spinelli spat back.

Shannon's eyes flooded with tears and she fought for a voice. "You..."

"I what?"

Shannon closed her eyes. "You're the coldest and harshest person I ever met," she whispered. She put her hand over her mouth and turned and walked away from him.

Spinelli stared after her. Her words sliced through his heart like a knife.

Chapter Six

Spinelli shuffled his feet in the direction of his precinct. He walked up behind Walker and Marsh as they stared at their Santa board. Spinelli cocked his head to the side and pulled his eyebrows together. "Is that an elf?" he asked as he stepped closer to the board to get a better look at the newly added photo of a murder victim wearing a short green smock with tights and green shoes that curled up at the toes.

The photo of the elf hung next to the pictures of Santa Claus.

Marsh continued to rub his fingers over his unshaven chin. "Yeah, that's an elf all right. The mall security guards found him early this morning while on their rounds."

"What do we know?" Spinelli asked.

"Same as Santa, a bullet to the back of the head and no identification on him. Mall security identified him as Aaron Reed, twenty-three, part-time college student," Marsh replied.

Walker picked up a file from his desk, flipped it open, and took a moment to scan the contents. He closed the file and looked over at Spinelli as he continued to study the pictures and information on the board. "Spinelli, tell me about this Shannon O'Hara."

Spinelli tore his gaze from the board and looked at Walker. The palms of his hands started to sweat as he thought about how to answer his question. "She's beautiful and smart. She's got the palest and softest looking skin, and eyes of an angel. I've never seen such bright emerald green eyes." Spinelli lost himself in thoughts of Shannon for a moment. "But she hates me. She absolutely hates me and the harder I try the worse it gets."

Spinelli paused, looked down at his feet, and then wondered if he really just said all that out loud.

Walker let out a chuckle that snapped Spinelli back to reality.

"What?" Spinelli asked.

"The great Spinelli is smitten by a woman who hates him. What's the matter there, buddy, off your game a bit? Oh, this is good. Did you hear that, Marsh? It sounds as if the great Spinelli is losing his touch with the ladies." Walker flashed a cocky smile. Spinelli shook his head. "Can we just stick to the issue at hand, the dead Santa and elf?"

"That's what I'm trying to do," Walker replied "It seems your little girlfriend upstairs knows both the victims and now that you guys are back we're going to have a little chat with her."

"What...how?" Spinelli cleared his throat, realigned his thoughts, and started over again. "What does Shannon have to do with any of this? Why do you need to speak to her?"

"Your little green eyed angel happens to play the role of Santa's little helper at the mall, however, she hasn't worked since last Sunday so I don't know if she even knows that her two buddies are dead. At any rate we need to get her down here."

"Spinelli!" Captain Jackson screeched from her office doorway, "in my office, now!"

Spinelli's body quivered at the sound of her voice. A sharp pain shot through his temples. He squeezed his eyes shut briefly, then spun on his heel and headed toward her office.

"Shut the door and sit down," Jackson hissed.

Jackson opened her desk drawer and retrieved a bottle of Tylenol. She dumped two tablets into her hand and put the bottle back. She flashed her angry dark brown eyes at Spinelli. "You do this to me, you know," she said as she tossed the tablets into her mouth and chased them down with coffee.

"Got a call from Ms. Fontaine. It appears that Shannon is quite upset again this morning. I thought we came to an understanding yesterday. I thought you were going to just do as you were told. I thought we were going to just get through the next couple of weeks and then everything would go back to normal. Where did we go wrong? What the hell did you do to piss her off so much? And for God's sake, Spinelli, tell me you didn't sleep with her already."

Jackson's last comment angered Spinelli. He sprang to his feet, stepped toward her desk and stared down at her. "First of all, I am doing what she told me to do but things just got a little out of hand this morning. This assignment is bullshit, absolute bullshit." He pointed out the window as he continued to speak, "We've got killers out there to apprehend and I'm wasting my time riding around with Social Services taking care of all this touchy-feely crap. And furthermore, it's nobody's business who I do and don't sleep with."

"Sit down, Spinelli."

Spinelli sat. He folded his arms over his chest, his jaw knotted so tight his ears started to hurt. Uncomfortable silence filled the Captain's office.

Jackson broke the silence. "I told Fontaine again that you're it. You are all we can spare right now. I assured her you would be on your best behavior. We'll get through the holiday season and then things will return to normal. Am I clear?"

"Yes."

Jackson pointed out her office window and Spinelli turned his head to look in that same direction. He saw Walker leading Shannon through the maze of desks toward the interview room. Marsh followed. Marsh caught Spinelli's attention, nodded toward Shannon, and mouthed the word "hot" while displaying the look of a starving lion on his face.

Spinelli sprang to his feet, took two steps toward Jackson's office door, and then looked back at her as if asking for permission to leave.

She met Spinelli's gaze and shook her head. "No, sit. Shit. Christ, Spinelli, don't do this to me. I don't have time for this shit."

"What, what shit? You said I should help Walker and Marsh with the Santa investigation. I need to be in that interview room," Spinelli snapped as he frantically shifted his glance back and forth between Shannon and Jackson.

Jackson blew out a sigh. "I don't think it's a good idea for you to be in there with her right now."

Spinelli opened his mouth to speak but she cut him off, "I wasn't born yesterday. I recognize that hungry look." Jackson paused and without breaking eye contact with Spinelli, she shook her head. "You certainly picked a fine time."

Chapter Seven

Spinelli paced the squad room. He ran his sweaty palms over his thighs, his heart raced and sharp pains danced through his head. He desperately needed to be in the interview room. He needed to know what Shannon knew about the murders, if anything. He couldn't imagine how anyone so sweet and thoughtful could be tangled up in anything as sordid as murder.

Finally, the door to the interview room swung open and Spinelli saw Shannon step out. Marsh and Walker followed. His heart skipped a beat when he saw her. He wanted nothing more than to reach out to her and wrap her in his arms. She looked exhausted. She blotted her teary red-stained eyes with a tissue, smearing the mascara further down her cheeks.

Spinelli had witnessed a lot of performances by the accused in his day but he knew deep down that she wasn't acting. He knew she didn't have anything to do with the deaths of Roland Hudson and Aaron Reed; she was just too pure.

Shannon stepped toward Spinelli and looked up at him through her long thick lashes with her big tear-filled emerald green eyes. She sniffled, "My friends…my friends were murdered."

Spinelli stepped toward her, closing the gap between them. He reached for her but she stepped back. "I'll be in my office, Detective. I won't need your services until later this afternoon."

He stared after her as she walked away. For the first time ever he felt rejected. But he found the rejection bothered him less than the fact that she hurt. He wanted to help her. He wanted to hold her and comfort her.

Marsh slapped Spinelli on his shoulder blade. "Ooh, that was cold, buddy. You're not kidding. She hates you."

"Shut up. Just shut the hell up!" Spinelli barked.

Spinelli turned to Walker. "Did she provide any insight as to who murdered Hudson and Reed?"

"I don't think she has a clue and Marsh verified her alibi while I talked with her."

A blanket of anger fell over Spinelli and he got in Walker's face. "Her alibi! You can't possibly think she's got anything to do with this!"

Walker took a step back. "Hey, pal, she knew both the vics and she worked with them where they were murdered. I'm only doing my job."

Spinelli pinched the bridge of his nose. He squeezed his eyes shut briefly and drew in slow deep breaths before dropping his hand to his side. "Sorry, Walker, I understand. You were right to take that approach. Out of curiosity, what's her alibi? How does she spend her evenings?"

Marsh cut in. "Well, your sweet little thing is exactly that. Both nights she was at St. Mary's church helping the Sisters with their Christmas Toys for Tots Program. Sister Mary verified that Shannon was there from 7:00 p.m. until shortly before midnight."

A wide smirk grew across Marsh's face.

"What, what's that smirk for?" Spinelli asked.

Marsh chuckled. "She is so not your type of woman."

* * * *

Shannon tossed her tear-dampened tissue into the garbage can and retrieved another from the tissue box on her desk. She pressed the tissue to her eyes to absorb the remaining tears.

The sound of heavy footsteps drew her attention causing her to look up and glance at the doorway. "Hi Anna."

"My God, are you okay? I heard what happened to Santa and the Elf, and I heard they just questioned you downstairs. Is that true?"

Shannon's emotions ran rampant throughout her causing her body to quiver. Her anger, hurt and grief all jockeyed for placement. Anger won. "That son of a bitch, he did this to me!"

Anna cocked her head to the side. "What? Who are you talking about?"

"Spinelli, that jerk!"

"Shannon, just calm down and take a breath then tell me what you mean."

Shannon stared into Anna's warm eyes and took a couple of deep breaths in an attempt to calm her racing heart. Her mind wrestled to place her thoughts in order.

"Detective Spinelli, he did this on purpose. For some reason he hates me. He's been an absolute jerk since he walked through my doorway. It's because of him Detectives Marsh and Walker questioned me about the murders of Roland and Aaron. I don't know what his problem is, he's just a dick!"

Anna sat down in the chair opposite Shannon's desk and leaned forward aligning her eyes with Shannon's. "Are you hearing yourself? I'm sure Detective Spinelli is not doing this just to make you miserable..."

"He is, Anna. You don't know him. He completely defies me when we're on a call. He doesn't know shit about what we deal with everyday yet he keeps overstepping his bounds and screws everything up! If you would have witnessed his behavior on the Washington and Smith calls you would understand what I'm talking about."

Anna leaned back in her chair and raked her hand through her graying hair. "Shannon, I think there's something you should know about Detective Spinelli."

"What, that he's really not human and his heart is made of stone?"

Anna shook her head. "Wow, you are torqued."

Shannon could feel her cheeks heating up. She suddenly felt embarrassed about the accusations she made about Spinelli. "I'm sorry, I am upset, but it's no reason for me to spout off to you. What is it I should know about Detective Spinelli?"

Anna leaned forward in her chair. "I just spoke with Captain Jackson in regard to getting a replacement for him, and well, he's all they have to spare right now. Jackson's not happy about it either, loaning out her best homicide detective to any other department, but apparently his partner just retired so he's the only one flying solo right now and all the others are loaded with open cases..."

"Can't they just shift him around and free up someone else?" Shannon interrupted.

"I asked the same question and apparently it's just not that simple."

"Oh."

Anna glanced about the room as she nibbled on her chapped bottom lip.

"Is there more? You look like you want to say more," Shannon asked.

Anna met Shannon's gaze and gave a slight nod. "Yeah, there is more I think you should know. You see, Detective Spinelli is actually quite aware of what we deal with day in and day out in our department."

"What? You could have fooled me," Shannon interrupted as she rolled her eyes.

"Shannon."

"Sorry."

"He's lived it, Shannon. Detective Spinelli grew up in the system. When he was real young he'd been passed around from foster home to foster home when he wasn't living with his drug addicted mother who supported her habit by prostituting herself."

Shannon's lips parted to speak but she closed them before any words escaped.

Anna continued. "When Detective Spinelli was sixteen his mother died of a drug overdose. He doesn't even know who is father is. Anyhow, he lived on the streets for a while making a living by card sharking and pool hustling until he woke up one day and decided to change his life. He finished high school and put himself through college all on his own." Anna offered a slight smile and shook her head. "Maybe this assignment is just a little too close to home for him."

Shannon placed her elbows on her desk and rested her head in her hands for a few moments, absorbing what she'd just heard. She lifted her head and met Anna's gaze again. "Is there more?"

"Well, I can tell Captain Jackson favors him a bit, maybe even mothers him a bit. She kept telling me over and over again what a great detective he is. She also mentioned that his partner, Mad Dog Maxwell, retired this week. I guess Mad Dog's been somewhat of a father figure to him."

Shannon sighed. Anna's eyes stayed fixed on her. "I feel like such an idiot. I wish I would have known this before. I was so rude to him downstairs after my interview with Detectives Walker and Marsh. He was trying to be nice to me and I totally snubbed him."

"Don't beat yourself up. You didn't know," Anna replied with a soft reassuring smile.

Shannon shook her head. "No, I didn't know but I should have been nicer to him anyway, professional courtesy. But I can't seem to help myself, for some reason he just infuriates me."

Chapter Eight

With reluctance Spinelli headed in the direction of Shannon's office. It was nearly 2:00, time for their next call. He rapped his knuckle on her office doorframe and she looked up at him from behind her desk. A ripple of relief flowed through his body when he noticed the corners of her mouth twitching upward, moving slowly and perhaps forced, but they were still moving in the right direction. He waited patiently for her smile. It took a bit but it did surface.

"Good afternoon, Detective Spinelli."

He returned her smile. "Good afternoon, Miss O'Hara."

The formalities struck him oddly but he went with it in an effort to not rock the boat and keep peace.

He took a seat in one of the guest chairs opposite her desk and sat quietly as he watched her pick up a legal sized envelope from the top of a tall stack of mail. She sliced the envelope open with a long plastic letter opener. She set both the letter and the opener down on her desk and turned her attention back to him. "I'm sorry but I meant to call you before you came up here this afternoon. Our home visit for this afternoon has been rescheduled for next week so I don't have anything for you on the docket for the remainder of the day."

A blanket of relief fell over Spinelli. He wouldn't have to go on another one of these awful calls for a couple of days but the relief was quickly chased off by disappointment. He found himself wanting to spend time with her but now that opportunity disappeared as well. He stood. "No problem, I'll be downstairs working on the Santa and Elf case. Call if you need me."

"Okay."

Spinelli stepped into the hall outside her office before he heard her loud gasp. He spun on his heel and stepped back into her office to find her staring down at what appeared to be an eight by ten photo. She held the photo in her right hand and the legal sized envelope in her left hand. He watched as she dropped the envelope and used her left hand to help steady the shaking photo. She pulled the photo closer to her eyes.

"What is it a picture of?" he asked as he stepped around her desk and behind her to get a better look. Spinelli stared down at a glossy of Shannon and Santa, and several elves, including Aaron Reed. In the photo, Santa sat on a large red velvet chair. The elves and Shannon surrounded him.

Shannon shifted her attention from the photo to Spinelli who stood behind her, looking over her shoulder. "It's a promotional photo we took at the mall last week."

Spinelli could easily see the sadness flood her bright emerald green eyes. She turned her attention back to the photo. Her shoulders slumped. "Seven of us in the photo, and now two are gone," she whispered.

"I'm sorry, Shannon."

Shannon set the photo on her desk and picked up the small yellow square sticky note stuck to her desktop calendar. She reached up and handed it to Spinelli. "This was stuck to the photo."

He took the note from her. The note read, *"Shannon, Be careful of the company you keep, things are not always as they seem. Roland."*

He scanned the note again and then looked down at Shannon.

"I don't know what he's talking about. I don't know who he means," Shannon blurted in an unsteady voice, shaking her head.

Spinelli glanced at the envelope the photo came in. The envelope showed no return address and the date stamp happened to be the same day Roland Hudson's body was found. He placed the note in front of her. "Shannon, do you recognize this handwriting? Is it Roland's?" he asked in a calm controlled voice in effort to not rattle her any more than she already was.

She studied the note. "I don't know. I don't recall if I ever saw anything Roland wrote."

"Had you spent time with Roland?"

"What do you mean?"

"I mean, were you friends? Did you do anything together? How well did you know him?"

Shannon thought for a moment. "I really didn't know him all that well. He was just a nice old man who played Santa Claus at the mall. I only ever saw him when we worked together the past couple of seasons."

Spinelli shifted his eyes back to the photo. "How about the other people in the photo? Who are they and how well do you know them?"

Shannon stared at the photo for a moment. "Outside of working with them I never see them. All I know about them is their names and the fact they are college students."

A monstrous wave of adrenaline rippled through Spinelli's veins moving his senses into "full alert" mode and a tsunami of questions flooded his mind. Did Roland really send the photo and message? If so, who, and what, exactly was he trying to warn her about? If Roland didn't send the package, who did? And, how much danger was she really in?

Spinelli looked down and stared into Shannon's big innocent naïve eyes. Unfortunately, he knew the answer to the most pertinent question. *Two murders equal a lot of danger.*

Chapter Nine

Spinelli stood in front of the mirror and looked at his arms as they stuck out beyond the fat suit he just fastened to himself. He turned sideways to view himself in the mirror before bending over to pull up the red velvet pants. The enormous gut-roll made the task nearly impossible. He caught his breath then bent over to pull on the big black boots he needed to wear, again a near to impossible undertaking.

He reached into his locker and pulled out a matching plush red velvet coat trimmed with white fur. He threw the coat around his shoulders and buttoned it. The coat fit snugly around his midsection. Next, he grabbed a wide black belt with a big gold buckle, flung it around his waistline, and fastened it on the last notch. From the shelf in the locker, he retrieved a wig with long white wavy hair, and a red velvet hat trimmed with white fur and tassel at the top. He tugged the wig over his head until it felt snug then he fastened on the matching beard. Instantaneously the beard caused his nose and face to itch.

Spinelli turned to face the mirror once again. He couldn't help but wonder how he came to be wearing a Santa suit at the mall. He wanted to be an elf but there were no elf positions available and Human Resources told him that there's no such thing as a six foot-two elf. As he stared at his ridiculous self in the mirror, he could hear Captain Jackson's laugh echo throughout his head. He recalled the words she said to him the day before, "Maybe playing Santa will do you some good. You know, soften you up a bit."

He took one last look at himself in the mirror. He reached up under his beard and scratched his itchy chin. "Well, working a homicide undercover as Santa beats child recovery and placement any day," he whispered to his reflection.

Spinelli strode out of the employee locker room and into the busy mall, his big belly swishing from side to side, as he walked. He didn't recall ever being in the mall on a Saturday during the Christmas holiday season before, and he knew it probably wouldn't ever happen again by choice. Hundreds of people, mostly women with their whiny kids in tow filled the mall.

He made his way through the crowd to Santa's village. He took in the sight of the wintery display as he walked through toward the red velvet chair. He glanced at the long line of children waiting for him. Panic rippled through his body.

Spinelli walked past the snowy field of colorful eight-foot candy canes and passed by the red sleigh overflowing with presents. He stepped onto the low platform, which housed his chair and took a seat. He glanced to the left where a couple of elves stood wearing their green smocks and tights, as well as, their pointy green hats and matching shoes which curled up at the toes. They whispered amongst themselves in front of the fifteen-foot Christmas tree decorated with large silver and gold ornaments and big red bows. Glancing up he took notice of the large sparkly silver star perched at the top of the tree. He shifted his gaze toward the line of children who anxiously waited to see him. *Good God, how did I end up here?*

A soft feminine voice rang in his ears, "Good afternoon, Santa. How are you today?"

Spinelli glanced in the direction of the voice to find Shannon, his little Santa's helper. The sight of her caused his heart to beat out of control. Never in his life had he seen anything as beautiful as the sight he saw now. He slowly eyed her from top to bottom starting with the big candy cane striped bow that held her thick long wavy ponytail in place. Some of her loose red curls dangled down over the side of her face and around her neck, resting softly on her shoulders. The white furry trim of her scoop neck velvet dress lay upon her chest just low enough allowing him to catch a glimpse of the tops of her small pale breasts. A wide black belt equipped with a big shiny gold buckle snuggled her dress to her slim waist, causing him to take note of her hourglass figure. Lowering his eyes further, he saw how the white furry trim on the bottom of her dress fell several inches above her knees exposing her slim but shapely legs.

He raised his eyes to meet hers. He locked in on her gaze. She took a step toward him, pulled a frown, and squinted, as if trying to figure out his identity. He quickly released his gaze. He suddenly felt the need to keep his identity a secret from her.

Spinelli watched as Shannon approached the line of children. She extended her arm toward the first little boy in line and he took her hand. "What is your name?" she asked the boy as she walked with him toward Spinelli.

"Matthew."

Shannon and Matthew walked up to Spinelli and stood right in front of him. Matthew looked up at him with his big brown eyes. Spinelli easily detected the fear in them. With as scared as Matthew seemed, Spinelli knew Matthew's fear level couldn't begin to compare to his own as he realized he didn't know the slightest thing about playing Santa or what to do with Matthew and the other fifty kids in line behind him. Spinelli flashed his confused gaze in Shannon's direction and almost as if she read his thoughts, she took charge of the situation. She looked down at Matthew. "Do you want to climb up on Santa's lap and tell him what you want for Christmas?"

Matthew nodded his little head. Shannon reached down, scooped him up, and placed him on Spinelli's lap then she crouched down in front of them and kept her eyes aligned with Matthew's. Spinelli still wasn't sure what to do. He could feel the sweat beading up on his upper lip and temples. His perspiration caused his face to itch even more under his strap-on beard. It took every bit of strength he could muster not to tear the beard off his face and scratch his chin raw.

Shannon shifted her gaze from Matthew's to Spinelli's and quietly mouthed, "Ho, ho, ho." Shear panic ran through his veins as she coaxed him along. He looked down at Matthew, sucked in a deep breath and let it out with a mighty and cheerful "Ho, ho, ho." The authenticity even surprised Spinelli. Matthew's eyes went wide and a smile grew across his chubby little face as he began to rattle off his extensive Christmas list.

Four hours later, the mother of the last child in line worked desperately to coax her daughter to climb up on Santa's lap, give him her Christmas list, and get her photo taken. After several failed attempts, the woman simply scooped her daughter up and planted her on Spinelli's lap. The little girl shifted her terrified blue-eyed gaze to Spinelli's and upon contact, she immediately started wailing. She slid down his leg to get off his lap but not before she peed her pants. Spinelli sprang to his feet as he realized what happened. The wetness penetrated through his plush red velvet pants causing his pant leg to stick to his skin. He wanted to swear a blue streak, but contained himself in front of those who remained in the Santa village.

Chapter Ten

Spinelli sauntered toward the employee locker room. Though anxious to lose the hot, itchy, and wet Santa suit, he slowed down to trail the elves and eavesdrop. Maybe he'd hear something he could use to nab the killer. But no, they droned on about semester finals and griped about having to work at the mall for the holidays. *Poor kids*, he thought as he did a mental eye roll.

Once in the locker room Spinelli kept listening while he peeled off the Santa suit. Still nothing important. He glanced at the soggy trousers. *Damn this is disgusting. What the hell is wrong with kids today?* With any luck, the drycleaners would be open in the morning and he could get the urine-polluted Santa suit cleaned before his shift tomorrow night.

He stuffed the suit into his duffel bag and slung it over his shoulder. He rounded the corner of the locker row to find the elves and a couple of security guards still talking among themselves. They stopped talking when they saw him looking at them. "Need something?" one elf asked.

Spinelli eyed each elf again while his mind worked to place each of them in their respective spots in the photo Shannon received in the mail. He needed something from them all right. He needed to know what they knew about the murders of Hudson and Reed.

Spinelli shrugged. "No not really. Just on my way out."

"You're a little young to be playing Santa Claus, don't ya think?" one of the young security guards teased.

He shrugged again. "A job's a job. Just need a little extra cash."

"Well, you must be desperate for cash to take a job as Santa," one elf said.

Spinelli tilted his head to the side and cocked a brow. "Why do you say that?"

"Well, it's not like you enjoy it. You're the worst Santa I've ever seen," the elf commented as he chuckled. "You looked stiff as a board all day and when that kid peed on you I thought you were going to have the holy big one."

Spinelli chose to ignore the elf's comments, chuckled, and continued to chat with them and security guards. He wanted to get to know them a bit and find out if they knew anything about the murders of Hudson and Reed. As he probed them he couldn't help but notice the nervous glances being exchanged between the elves and security guards, as if trying to communicate a pact of silence. Finally, one of the security guys broke off. "We need to get back on watch. See ya'll later."

Spinelli followed the security guards and the elves out of the locker room to find Shannon waiting outside the door. She waited for the others to pass by before she spoke to him. "What are you doing here?"

"Playing Santa."

"Yes, I see that. But why?"

"Because I want to and it's fun being with all the children," Spinelli choked out.

Shannon rolled her eyes. "Yeah right. You really looked like you enjoyed yourself and knew what you were doing today," she commented sarcastically.

Shannon stopped talking and eyed Spinelli. He watched her as her pale cheeks turned even whiter and as her eyes began to flood with tears. Her breaths grew quick and shallow. "Oh my God," she whispered. Then she threw her hand over her mouth.

He took a step toward her and she quickly stepped back. He took another step toward her and again she stepped back, pressing her back against the wall.

"Stay away from me! Just stay away."

"What? What's the matter?" he asked.

"You're here to keep an eye on me aren't you? You and Detectives Marsh and Walker still think I had something to do with the murders don't you? They were my friends. How could you even think that?"

"No, that's not it at all. Just let me explain," Spinelli said as he took another step closer to her.

Shannon lifted her hand and placed it on his chest, stopping him from stepping any closer to her. Her lips quivered and the tears that flooded her eyes began to roll down her pale cheeks. "Don't."

Shannon's knees grew weak and she slowly slid down the wall until her butt rested on the floor. She wrapped her arms around her knees and buried her face between her chest and knees smothering her sobs.

Spinelli dropped his duffel bag to the floor and took a seat next to her. He slung his arm around her shoulders and pulled her close to his side. He didn't know what else to do. Comforting crying women did not come easily to him.

After several minutes of uncontrollable crying, she appeared to pull herself together. She lifted her head and used her sleeve to wipe away the remaining tears that clung to her cheeks.

Without a word, she rose to her feet and began walking away from Spinelli. He sprang to his feet, slung his duffel bag over his shoulder, and kept pace at her side. "Let me walk you to your car."

"I didn't drive here." Her eyes focused ahead, not on him.

"How did you get here?"

"Bus," she replied coolly.

"The bus," he repeated.

Shannon stopped in her tracks, perched her hands on her hips, and stared at him. "Yes, the bus. You can never get a parking spot in the ramp this time of year so it's just easier to take the bus to the front door. Is that okay with you, Detective Spinelli? Are you finished with the inquisition? Can I go in peace now?" Her tone was so sharp it made his blood run cold.

Spinelli found himself stammering. He'd never known a woman to push him to the state of mumbling before and he didn't like it. He didn't like it one bit, yet though she appeared to want nothing to do with him, he felt a compelling need to make sure she got home safely. "You know what...can we just start over? All I want to do is make sure you get home safely. Something is going on here and until I get to the bottom of it I just...I just want to make sure you're safe so I'd like to drive you home, okay?"

Shannon pressed her hand over her mouth. She inhaled deeply and stared down at the floor. Then she lifted her gaze to meet Spinelli's, dropping her hand to her side. "I'm sorry I was so rude. This whole thing is just a little more than I can handle right now. I really liked Roland. He was such a kind and sweet old man. I can't think of any possible reason why someone would kill him. It just doesn't make sense. He was kind to everyone."

Spinelli absently pressed his fingers to his chest as if trying to shield his heart from the stabbing pain penetrating from Shannon's grief filled eyes to his. "I'll get to the bottom of this. We'll get the answers. But for now, please just let me drive you home."

Shannon nodded and walked along with him toward the mall's parking ramp. Silence and darkness filled the mall. Only a few store attendants lingered about as they put the closing touches on their stores. Spinelli eyed them all as he walked by wondering if any of them knew anything about the murders or if they themselves had anything to do with the murders of Hudson and Reed.

From the second floor balcony, Spinelli looked down toward the Greek restaurant on the first floor. A Closed sign hung in the window. The two elves and two security guards he talked to earlier appeared to be waiting by the retractable metal security gate blocking the entrance to the restaurant. He slowed his pace and watched the men and the entrance to the restaurant. He took in every detail. After a moment, the gate opened, exposing a heavy-set dark haired, dark skinned man. Spinelli figured the man stood about five-foot-ten and weighed about two-hundred and fifty pounds. He placed his age at about fifty-five or so. A little muscle trailed the heavy-set dark haired man. The muscle consisted of two tall well-built younger gentlemen dressed all in black, maybe in their early thirties. Both men appeared to be of the same descent as the older gentleman, perhaps Mediterranean. The elves and security guards entered the restaurant and the musclemen closed the gate behind them.

"That's Loukas the Greek. He owns the restaurant," Shannon said as Spinelli continued to stare down at the restaurant entrance.

Spinelli shifted his gaze to Shannon. "What?"

"That guy you were staring at is Loukas the Greek. He owns the restaurant," she repeated.

"Oh. I wonder what they're doing in there after hours."

Shannon glanced down toward the restaurant. "They play cards."

"Really?"

Shannon shrugged. "I've heard the security guys talk about how they play poker in there after hours."

"Hmm," Spinelli replied as he continued to walk toward the parking structure. He desperately wanted to check out their game, their business, but he put that on hold to deal with his immediate priority, Shannon, and getting her home safely.

Chapter Eleven

Spinelli parked his truck in the only vacant stall in the parking lot of Shannon's apartment complex. He cut the engine and glanced about the area surrounding the two-story brick building. When he deemed it safe, he turned his attention to Shannon who sat silent in the passenger seat staring through the windshield.

"Shannon," Spinelli whispered.

The second he said her name her body flinched and she gasped for air.

"Sorry, I didn't mean to startle you but you're home."

"It's okay. Thanks for the ride," she replied as she nervously reached for the door handle.

Spinelli flung his door open and slid out of the truck. He raced to the other side of the vehicle and reached Shannon's side just as she shut the passenger door. "I'll walk you to your door."

"Thank you but you don't need to. I'll be fine," she replied.

Spinelli simply ignored her and continued to walk with her. When they reached the front door Shannon ran her fingers over the numeric touchpad and the door unlocked. He followed her through the doorway and the common area, which housed a wall of mailboxes. He continued to follow her, as she turned left in the long narrow corridor. She paused and looked back at him. "I'm fine. You don't need to bother yourself any longer. I think I can manage from here."

He strapped on his lady-killer grin. "It's no bother." He continued to follow her to her apartment door.

Shannon fumbled with her key. Her nervous hands struggled even more as she tried to insert the key into the slot.

Spinelli reached over and took the key from her hand. "I'll get that for you."

The soft quick brush of her hand against his caused the blood in his veins to heat up just short of boiling.

Spinelli turned toward the sound of a door opening behind him to find a little old lady standing in the doorway of the apartment directly across the hall from Shannon's. "Is that you dear?" the woman asked.

Shannon spun around to face the woman. "Yes, Mrs. Finch, it's me. We didn't wake you did we?"

"Oh no dear, me and Sister are just watching the news. Well Sister's watching, and I'm listening. I heard you come home so I thought I'd just give you my grocery list tonight and see how your day was at the mall. Were there lots of children visiting Santa today?"

Spinelli watched Shannon smile as she spoke with Mrs. Finch. "Yes, the mall was packed and the line of children was endless for a while."

Mrs. Finch smiled. "Oh what fun, I love this time of year."

The conversation paused and Spinelli continued to look at Mrs. Finch as she stood in the doorway in her pink bathrobe belted at the waist. Small black curlers held her steel gray hair in place. Mrs. Finch's eyes widened and her face lit up as if someone turned a light bulb on within her. She stepped out of the doorway and into the hall and turned her head from Shannon to Spinelli. "Did you say 'we' dear?"

Before Shannon could reply, Mrs. Finch turned her head back in the direction of her apartment and yelled with her fragile voice. "Sister, come quick. Shannon's got company and he smells like a hot one."

Spinelli couldn't help but smile at Mrs. Finch's comment and when he flashed his eyes in Shannon's direction he caught her eye roll. The shuffle of feet drew his attention back toward Mrs. Finch's apartment door. Another little old lady surfaced in the doorway. Not only did she look just like the first little old lady, she dressed the same as well.

The second little old lady flashed a smile in his direction and then looked at Shannon. "Who's your friend, dear?"

Shannon gestured toward Mrs. Finch and her sister and looked at Spinelli, "Nick Spinelli, these are my neighbors, Sally Finch and Sarah

Knight. Mrs. Finch and Mrs. Knight, this is Nick Spinelli."

Mrs. Finch reached toward Spinelli and he took her small cold boney shriveled hand in his. "I'm pleased to meet you, Mrs. Finch."

Mrs. Finch's smile grew, nearly stretching from ear to ear. She let out a giggle and turned her head toward her sister. "Large warm hands, smells good, does he look as hot as he feels and smells?" she asked in a stage whisper.

Mrs. Knight flashed a wink in Spinelli's direction, smiled, leaned toward her sister and whispered, "Oh, he's a looker alright, tall, dark and handsome. Mysterious eyes, the kind a woman can get lost in. Looks to be pretty fit too, Sister. Too bad you can't see this one, he's a delight."

Spinelli kept most of his attention focused on the sisters but he took a glance at Shannon out of the corner of his eye. A bright shade of red began consuming her pale colored skin rising upward from her neck.

"Come on, Sister, let's leave these kids alone to go about their business."

"We don't have any business," Shannon immediately piped up. "I mean Mr. Spinelli just gave me a ride home from work. We're not really…"

Mrs. Finch interrupted Shannon mid-sentence. "Shannon, dear, why don't you share some of those delicious gingerbread cookies you baked with your friend? She's an excellent baker, Mr. Spinelli."

He couldn't help himself, "I'd love to try them. Gingerbread cookies are my favorite."

Spinelli wished the ladies a good night and turned to follow Shannon into her apartment.

"What do you think you're doing?" Shannon asked him.

"I'm getting my cookies."

He reached for the door behind him and heard the sisters whispering.

"It's about time that sweet girl gets a man in her life."

"You're right, Sister, her clock is ticking. Poor thing."

The door clicked shut. Spinelli stifled his chuckle and pressed on about the cookies.

Shannon rolled her eyes and shook her head. "Fine, I'll give you some cookies and that's all you're getting. Then will you please just leave?" she asked as she spun on her heel and headed toward the kitchen shedding her coat along the way.

Spinelli easily sensed her discomfort and he blamed it on her unwanted attraction to him. He couldn't help but want to add to her discomfort, tease her just a bit. "Are you normally this rude to all the guests you invite in for cookies?"

Shannon turned to face Spinelli. She flashed him a scowl and took a moment to conjure up her response. "Excuse me but I don't recall inviting you in for cookies. What I recall is you rudely inviting yourself in for cookies."

Spinelli fought to keep from smiling. He liked the way she tried to cover her nervousness as she spoke to him. The conscious attempt made her voice deeper and even sexier than normal. With a voice like that he thought for sure she could double as a one nine-hundred operator.

Shannon quickly turned again and headed in the direction of the kitchen. Spinelli followed with his eyes fixed on her backside. She probably had no clue how sexy she looked in her skimpy Santa helper outfit. Didn't notice the elves ogling her all night either; the thought of it stirred the jealous juices inside him.

Spinelli shrugged off his coat and flung it over the back of one of the two counter-height stools situated at the kitchen island. He pulled the stool out and took a seat. He figured he could get away with making himself comfortable and staying for a while because he knew she would want to prove him wrong about her being rude. And he knew she wouldn't be able to live with herself if someone thought of her as being rude.

Shannon turned to face him, a clear plastic bag full of cookies gripped in her fist. She reached over the counter and handed them to him. He took them from her and set them on the counter. He undid the twist-tie and pulled one from the bag.

"What are you doing?" she asked.

Spinelli shifted his eyes from his bag of cookies and looked up at Shannon. "I'm eating my cookies."

She narrowed her gaze but said nothing. From the look on her face, he knew he had her. She was just too nice to kick him out and most important, he knew that deep down she felt an attraction to him. He knew she didn't want it to be so, but she was.

After a brief moment of silence, Shannon slipped into the mode Spinelli knew she would. "Would you like some milk with your cookies?"

Spinelli smiled. "Yes, please."

Shannon turned toward the refrigerator and opened it. She bent over and reached into the fridge to grab the jug of milk from the bottom shelf, exposing more of her shapely legs. Excitement penetrated throughout Spinelli's body, nearly caused him to choke. *God, she doesn't have a clue.*

She shut the refrigerator door and then reached up into the cupboard to retrieve two glasses, again, causing her little dress to rise up.

She poured a glass of milk for Spinelli and one for herself then she took a seat alongside him and grabbed a cookie.

Spinelli took a swig of his milk to chase down the cookie and then set the glass back on the counter top. He shifted his stool a bit in order to face Shannon. "What do you know about this card game? Did Hudson and Reed play?"

Shannon set the remainder of her cookie down on her plate and took a drink of her milk. She ran her tongue across her lips clearing away the remaining cookie crumbs and milk from them. The maneuver sent Spinelli's heart into overdrive. He willed her to do it again only this time he imagined himself capturing her tongue with his mouth. He imagined his tongue in a long slow dance with hers.

She answered his question, interrupting his fantasy. "I don't really know anything about the game. I've heard the college kids, you know, the elves, and the security guards talk about how they play cards in the Greek restaurant after the mall closes. I think they play poker. I would imagine that Aaron Reed played but I don't think Roland Hudson played."

"Do they play every night and do they play for money?"

Shannon thought for a moment. "I'm not sure if they play every night. I only work on the weekends and I know they play on the weekends and I definitely know they play for money. I've heard some of the elves talk about how they need to work for Loukas at times to pay off their debt. So here they are trying to earn extra cash for school and they need to work off their gambling debts."

"Do you know what they do to work off their gambling debts?"

Shannon responded with a slight shrug. "I just assumed they worked in the restaurant or something. I never really thought about it."

Spinelli finished his cookies and downed the last of his milk. He'd hoped it would take longer so he could spend more time with Shannon but the cookies were so good he just couldn't help but gobble them up—like he wanted to gobble her up but knew she wasn't ready for that yet. He figured her for the kind of woman that planned out every move in her life. She would take her time when it came to letting a man into it. As much as he wanted her right now he didn't mind the wait. She would be worth it.

He slid his stool back from the counter and stood. He pulled his coat from the back of the stool and flung it over his shoulders. "Well, it's getting late. Are you working at the mall tomorrow?" he asked, knowing the answer because he'd already checked the work schedule which hung in the employee break room.

"Yes, I work from five to nine," she replied as she rose from her stool and stood in front of Spinelli, staring up at him with her big green eyes.

"So I'll pick you up at about 4:30 then?" he asked hoping not to get any grief from her. Not only did he just desire to be with her he also wanted to keep an eye on her. He didn't know what was going on yet or why Hudson and Reed were both murdered at the mall and he feared for her safety.

Spinelli kept his eyes fixed on hers, as she appeared to debate her answer to his question. She blinked flirtatiously as a soft smile drew across her face. "So you're going to stick out the Santa thing at least another day?"

Spinelli returned her smile. "What are you saying? You don't think I make a good Santa?"

Shannon's soft sweet chuckle rang through his ears. "Oh, you're a natural, all right. I don't recall ever seeing a man look so horrified at the sight of children."

Her chuckle turned to full-blown laughter. "And when that little girl had an accident on your lap you looked like you were going to die right there on the spot."

Spinelli laughed deeply. He knew she was right. He had very little experience with children.

"Hopefully the drycleaners can do a rush job on my uniform tomorrow morning."

Shannon smiled. "I'm sure they'll give a little extra effort for Santa."

Shannon saw Spinelli to the door. He stepped through the doorway and turned toward her, his eyes fixed on hers. "I'll pick you up at 4:30 tomorrow."

"Okay. Goodnight."

Chapter Twelve

The next afternoon, Spinelli headed to Shannon's apartment to pick her up for work. By the time he parked his truck in the one available visitor parking spot he could see her already walking down the snow dusted sidewalk toward his truck. He quickly put the truck in park and slid out so he could open the passenger door for her. She smiled at him. Her plump red lips almost an invitation.

Spinelli kept his eyes on her as she climbed up into his truck so he could catch a glimpse of those great legs. He shut the door behind her, walked around the truck, and hopped onto the driver's seat.

As he drove toward the mall, he made small talk and inquired about her neighbors, Mrs. Finch and Mrs. Knight. Shannon explained that both ladies were widows and that they'd lived together in the apartment across the hall since way before she moved into the complex. Neither of them drove because Mrs. Finch is almost completely blind, she can only see shadows, and Mrs. Knight's vision is beginning to diminish as well. So, when they need to go grocery shopping, or anywhere else, she usually takes them. Unfortunately, they both outlived their children but they do have a few grandchildren scattered about the country.

Spinelli glanced over at Shannon as she talked about her neighbors. He'd never met anyone like her before. Never in his life did he ever meet anyone so kind and thoughtful, as well as, beautiful, smart, and sexy. The longer she spoke the faster his heart beat. He made up his mind right then and there he needed to make her his.

A Sunday, two weeks before Christmas, proved to be quite busy at the mall. So busy, in fact, that Spinelli couldn't find a parking spot. He dropped Shannon off at the entrance to Kohl's and he continued on driving around in the parking structure looking for an available spot. His second pass proved lucky.

Spinelli hurried to the employee locker room, strapped on his fat suit and buried it under his Santa suit and then hustled to the North Pole display where he found a line of children at least a mile long waiting for his arrival. He dreaded the next four hours. He hoped it wouldn't be as bad as the previous day. He took his seat in the velvet chair and nodded in the direction of the two elves. Out of the corner of his eye, he saw his little Santa helper appear from behind the candy cane field. Just like the day before, the sight of her in her short little red dress sucked the air right out of his lungs and no matter how hard he tried he couldn't seem to fill them.

Shannon walked up to Spinelli, smiled softly, and placed her hand lightly on his shoulder to get his attention. "Are you ready Santa?"

The touch of her hand sent a ripple of warmth flowing throughout his body. He worked hard to find a controlled voice. "Yes, I'm ready."

Like the day before, she strolled over to the eager children and began moving them toward him.

Spinelli glanced over the line. There were so many kids. Where did they all come from? A familiar face caught his attention. It was Lesha Washington. Her brother Darius stood next to her. The tall dark-haired woman he'd met two days earlier at the foster home held baby Christina on her hip. A young boy he didn't recognize stood next to her. Was that her child or another foster child as well?

Shannon plopped a little boy on Spinelli's lap. The enthusiastic little fellow rattled off his wish list before Santa even had a chance to ask for it.

Children came and went. With each passing child, Spinelli felt a bit more comfortable in this new role. It wasn't so bad. All he really had to do to make the kids happy was let out an occasional mighty "Ho, ho, ho" followed by a belly jiggling laugh, and the kids did the rest.

The Washington kids drew closer. They were laughing, all of them, even the foster mom. They seemed happy. Spinelli wondered if those kids had ever been truly happy in their short lives. If not, now maybe they stood a chance. The foster mom crouched down in front of Lesha. Lesha whispered something into her ear. The woman smiled, kissed her on the cheek, and hugged her before she stood up again. Lesha reached out and took the woman's hand. Darius held Lesha's other hand. They'd only been in foster care for a couple of days, yet something already seemed different about them.

A few more kids passed by Spinelli. Now it was the Washington kid's turn.

As they approached, Lesha zeroed in on Shannon. "Hi Ms. O'Hara."

Shannon smiled. "Well hello there Le…"

Spinelli cut her off, "Don't tell me. Is that Lesha Washington?"

Lesha's eyes widened and she flashed him a humungous smile. Darius slid behind her.

"Where did that little brother of yours go?" Santa asked as he leaned over and peeked around Lesha. He caught Darius' gaze. "Come on over here Darius and tell Santa what you want for Christmas."

"Go on, go tell Santa what you want," Lesha urged her little brother.

Darius walked up to Santa. Shannon lifted him up and placed him on Santa's lap. Spinelli caught and held his gaze. The fear in Darius' eyes faded. He smiled and asked for a fire truck before he slid off Santa's lap and ran back to his foster mom.

Spinelli looked at Lesha. She pointed at the other little boy with them. "Samuel can go next. He's been so excited all day to see you."

Was this how it was? Already the little mother hen at only seven years old. Spinelli's heart went out to her. He hoped she would get a childhood, the normal kind, where kids laugh and play, and where parents take care of their kids and love them. Something he never knew.

Samuel darted over to Santa and hopped up onto his lap and offered his Christmas list. Samuel finished quickly and scooted back down.

Spinelli looked at Lesha. She seemed to be studying him. She shifted her gaze to Shannon. Shannon stepped toward her, took her hand, and led her to Santa. Spinelli pulled her up onto his lap. Shannon stood by their side.

Lesha caught his gaze and held it, her eyes inquisitive. Did she know who he really was? How could she?

Spinelli softened his voice, "Well Lesha, I've had my eye you. It seems you've had a pretty tough year and through it all you've been a very good girl. And you've kept an eye on your little brother and sister, and took care of them. I'm very proud of you. Now tell me, what do you want for Christmas?"

She looked up at him with her big brown eyes. He decided in this instant that whatever this little girl wanted she was going to get. He'd run out tomorrow and buy it and make sure it made under her tree on Christmas morning.

Lesha brushed his hair back and whispered into his ear. A lump formed in his throat. He wasn't sure how to respond. He glanced at Shannon and caught her curious gaze. He'd tell her what Lesha asked for later, she'd need to know. He turned back to Lesha, "I'll see what I can do, Sweetheart."

She kissed him on the cheek and slid off his lap.

Spinelli stared after the foster family as they walked away. He'd give anything to make good on her Christmas wish; he knew how she felt. He'd been there himself in the past.

Four hours later, he wished for toothpicks to prop his eyelids open. He rose from his chair and sauntered toward the elves that stood by the display's Christmas tree as they ogled Shannon and made small talk with her. Spinelli's pure exhaustion did not prevent his jealous juices from finding their way to the surface.

Loukas, the Greek's muscleman, nudged his way between Spinelli and Shannon, scowled at Spinelli, then grunted in the direction of the elves. "You guys have fifteen minutes."

The elves' moods instantly turned somber and they ended their conversation and headed toward the employee locker room. Spinelli and Shannon followed close behind. Shannon slipped into the ladies locker room and Spinelli into the men's. He sat on the bench and began the difficult task of removing his black boots, considering the extreme gut roll of the fat suit he wore. He groaned during the maneuver drawing the attention of the elves.

"What the hell is muscleman's problem, cranky bastard?" Spinelli asked the elves.

The elves shifted their eyes from Spinelli to each other and looked as if urging each other to answer him. One of the elves shrugged his shoulders but neither said a word.

"You know, I could use a little extra cash for the holidays. How do you get into this nightly poker game I keep hearing about?" Spinelli continued.

He kept his eyes fixed on both elves and waited for a reply. Without a word, the smaller of the two elves hung his elf suit on a hook in his locker, shut the door, and pinched the padlock shut with his trembling fingers. The larger of the two elves stowed his elf suit in his locker, locked it, and then turned to face Spinelli. "I don't know what you're talking about."

He motioned for his fellow elf to follow and they left the locker room without looking back.

Spinelli finished shrugging out of his Santa suit and stuffed it into his duffel bag. He left the locker room to find Shannon waiting outside the door. "What did you say to those boys?" she asked.

"Nothing. Why? What happened?"

"Well they looked pretty frantic when they came out of the locker room and I heard one tell the other to just keep his mouth shut and that he'd figure a way out of it."

"What is 'It'?" Spinelli asked.

Shannon shook her head. "I don't know. They didn't say. They saw me standing here and stopped talking."

"Where did they go?" Spinelli asked as he walked briskly toward the edge of the second floor balcony so he could look down on the first floor of the mall. Sure enough, he saw the two elves. The muscleman at the Greek restaurant lifted the metal security gate and let the boys pass through. Spinelli quickly stepped back from the edge of the balcony to avoid being seen by the muscle but when he did so he bumped into Shannon. He hit her so hard she started to fall backwards. He reached out, grabbed her arm just above her elbow, and pulled her tightly to him to steady her.

"I'm sorry. Are you okay?"

"Yes, I'm fine."

Spinelli just stood there staring down into her big emerald green eyes, tightly gripping her arm. He tried to pull his gaze from hers but couldn't. He tried to free his hand from her arm but couldn't—it felt paralyzed. He debated kissing her. She looked like she wanted to be kissed but he couldn't dip his head. His mind willed his extremities to move but they wouldn't. He never in his entire life felt so tightly wound as he did right now. He feared that the slightest move would cause him to unravel completely.

"You're still on my foot," Shannon whispered, knocking Spinelli out of his trance.

"What?"

"My foot, you're standing on my foot."

Spinelli took a step back. "I'm sorry."

"It's okay."

"We better get going," Spinelli said as he turned and led her toward the parking ramp.

Spinelli opened the truck door for Shannon. Before climbing in she spun to face him. She fixed her warm green-eyed gaze on him. She had the most beautiful eyes.

I have to ask, "What did Lesha whisper to you?"

Spinelli thought about Lesha's Christmas wish. His body quivered. Goose bumps lined his arms. He cleared his throat. "She asked for a new mom and dad for her, and her brother and sister then maybe Darius wouldn't be scared and cry all the time." Spinelli paused. It was harder than he thought it would be to actually say the words. "She asked for a mom like you or the new foster mom, a mom that would love them and take care of them." His heartbeat quickened. Though it was only thirty degrees outside his cheeks were on fire. His heart ached.

Shannon placed her hand over her chest. Her eyes swam with tears. She lifted her hand to his cheek. "Those poor kids, they deserve so much more. No child deserves to live that way."

She held his gaze. The intensity of her stare frightened him. He knew she knew. Somehow she'd found out about his childhood. Sweat beaded on his upper lip. His comfort level plummeted. He needed to end this conversation. He hit the remote start button on his key fob. The engine roared.

Silence filled the vehicle during the drive back to Shannon's apartment. No matter how hard he tried, he couldn't clear his mind long enough to speak one sentence. When he wasn't thinking about Shannon, and the fact she knew his dirty little secret, thoughts of Lesha, and her Christmas wish, consumed him.

He parked his truck, slid out, scooted over to the passenger side door, and opened it for Shannon. He walked her to the front door and watched as she keyed in the numeric pass code. The door buzzed and Spinelli pushed it open and held it for her to pass through. He followed her to her apartment. No sooner did she place the key in the slot the door to the apartment across the hall from hers opened and Mrs. Finch stepped out.

"Good evening, dear."

"Hello, Mrs. Finch. How are you tonight?" Shannon asked.

"Oh, I'm good, good as it gets for a woman my age," Mrs. Finch replied as her lips rose upward into a wide smile. She glanced over her shoulder. "Sister, come quick. Shannon's home and her hot smelling friend from last night is here again."

Spinelli caught Shannon's eye roll, and was unable to refrain from smiling.

Spinelli could hear the shuffle of Mrs. Knight's feet seconds before she surfaced in the doorway. She glanced up at them. "Hello, Shannon. It's nice to see you again, Mr. Spinelli. Please forgive my sister. She's always been a little nosey and loose with her tongue."

Mrs. Knight turned her attention to her sister. "Come, Sister, leave the kids be and let them get on with their evening."

Shannon unlocked her apartment door and stepped through with Spinelli on her heels, he wanted in. He wanted to spend more time with her. Shannon spun around. "Thank you for seeing me home. I appreciate it. Have a good night."

Spinelli's mind raced. He tried to think of a way to get her to invite him in and for the first time in his life, not one good lady-killer line presented itself. Blank, his mind came up blank.

"Good night, Shannon, I'll see you in the morning."

"Oh, I've got court in the morning so I won't need you until after lunch."

"Okay, I'll come up to your office after lunch then."

Shannon's apartment door clicked shut. *Rejection, really?* Her rejection made him want her even more.

Chapter Thirteen

Shannon arrived at work at precisely 8:00 a.m. She flipped on the lights, deposited her briefcase on her desk, and set her coffee mug on top of the file cabinet. She stowed her purse in the file drawer, and then shrugged out of her coat and hung it on the coat tree.

As she reached over to retrieve her coffee mug, she paused to study the photo of her three nephews. Without conscious thought, she pressed a light kiss to the photo with the tip of her finger. "I miss you boys," she whispered out loud.

Shannon pulled open the second drawer of the file cabinet and shuffled through the alphabetical files until she reached the Clarkson file. She pulled it out, laid it on the top of the other files, and flipped it open. She studied the notes so she would be prepared for the 9:00 a.m. custody hearing. She paged through the paperwork and found a photo of the Clarkson children, James, age six and Katrina, age three. Shannon lifted the photo from the file and brought it closer to her eyes. *You poor kids.* Her heart grew heavy and a sharp pain shot through it. She closed her eyes; a tear rolled down her cheek. She couldn't help but feel sorry for the Clarkson children for all they were going through at their young ages, and for all the other children she dealt with on a daily basis going through similar situations.

Shannon's mind drifted away from thoughts of the Clarkson children to Spinelli. She wondered what he was like as a child. She wondered how many times a caseworker pulled his file from a drawer and recommended foster care for him. The events of Spinelli's life gave her hope, hope for the other children in the system. He made it out of the system and did well for himself. Maybe the Clarkson children will as well.

The Clarkson children had been removed from the home of their parents, Lamar and Chandra, because Lamar and Chandra had been busted for using and selling marijuana. The kids were placed in temporary foster care. The judge would determine today whether or not the kids would be released back into their parent's custody. Shannon glanced over toward the photo of her nephews. She picked up their photo, pressing it and the photos of the Clarkson children to her heart.

Shannon glanced down at her watch. It read 8:50. She put the photos back in their places. She tucked the file folder under her arm as she headed out of her office and toward the courtroom on the first floor.

She arrived in the courtroom at five minutes to nine. She took the aisle seat in the front row positioned immediately behind the children's appointed attorney. She glanced over to see Lamar and Chandra Clarkson sitting at a table with their appointed attorney. They looked like model citizens all decked out in their Sunday best, much unlike their mug shots stapled to the front of the manila file labeled 'Clarkson' which rested on her lap.

Shannon stared at the mug shot of Lamar. His matted coils of hair hung far beyond his shoulders and blocked much of his unshaven face, and though the photo was in black and white, she could easily make out his tie-dyed shirt. Her eyes shifted from the photo to Lamar who sat next to his attorney. Today he wore a maroon dress shirt and khakis. His head and face were now shaved clean. Shannon looked down at the photo of Chandra. Her short afro was pressed flat to her head on one side as if she'd just gotten out of bed and the dark circles under her eyes told the same story. She glanced over at Chandra who sat next to Lamar. She looked pretty today. Her hair was fluffed and the Cover Girl makeup worked its wonders. She wore dark brown dress pants and a hot pink sweater with pearl beads accenting the neckline. Shannon stared at both Lamar and Chandra. She hoped the visual front they were putting on today wouldn't fool the judge.

Shannon listened as James' school psychologist, Mrs. Charles, testified.

"Mrs. Charles, what is your position?" the children's attorney asked.

"I'm the school psychologist."

"How long have you worked in that position?"

"Nearly fifteen years."

"Have you been treating James Clarkson?"

"Yes."

"Tell us about James and his home environment."

Mrs. Charles glanced at Lamar and Chandra then shifted her eyes back to the attorney, "James is a textbook case of child neglect. He fends for himself and his little sister. He rarely speaks and has missed nearly fifty percent of the school days so far this year. His attendance has increased since he's been in foster care."

Both attorneys asked Mrs. Charles a few more questions then released her from the witness stand. Shannon's turn to testify came. Knowing her testimony would be crucial to the judge's decision about placing the children she paused briefly to gather her thoughts before answering each question.

"Counseling, both family and individual, was recommended when this case first crossed my desk. Rehab was also recommended for Lamar and Chandra," Shannon said from the witness stand. "None of the recommendations were taken."

The attorney guided the testimony along. "You've been a caseworker of record on this case for nearly a year."

"Yes."

"What is the current status?"

"As recently as a month ago Mr. Clarkson was arrested for possession of drug paraphernalia. It's been six months for Mrs. Clarkson. And again, neither has attended the recommended counseling or rehabilitation."

Lamar and Chandra groaned dramatically as Shannon spoke. Shannon refused to look at them, not wanting to give them the time of day. She fought to keep her concentration on her testimony, hoping not to inadvertently let the children down. Sometimes just the simplest mistake or miss-wording would send things awry and cause everything to spiral hopelessly out of control.

Shannon continued to answer questions about the children and the case file, and when the children's attorney finished his questioning Shannon prepared herself for the frustration of cross-examination.

"Are you aware that Mr. Clarkson has agreed to enter a rehabilitation program?" the Clarkson's court appointed attorney asked.

"Yes, I'm aware that he has agreed to enter a rehabilitation program just like the other two times in the past ten months when he agreed to enter but didn't."

"Lying bitch," Lamar yelled as he slammed his fists on the worn wooden table in front of him. All eyes shifted to him. His hardened face screamed with rage. *Poor Lamar. Is he having a tough day?* Shannon imagined part of his frustration was not that he may lose his children, but with the loss of his kids came the loss of his tax-payer supported income.

Judge Matthews lifted his hand and pointed his old shriveled boney finger in Lamar's direction. "Mr. Clarkson, if you can't control yourself you'll be removed."

Lamar grunted and stiffened his shoulders.

"Ms. O'Hara, have either Mr. or Mrs. Clarkson physically abused the children?" the Clarkson's attorney continued.

Shannon paused before she answered the question, knowing the fate of the children rested on her shoulders. "No, there have been no reports of physical abuse."

"Thank you Ms. O'Hara. That is all I have."

"But wait, one must consider the emotional abuse and neglect the children have suffered," Shannon squeaked out in a frantic voice as she glared in the direction of the Clarksons, and was completely ignored by their lawyer.

The judge dismissed Shannon from the witness chair. She stepped down and headed back to her seat. She feared she had failed the children. Anger rippled through her body and as she passed by the Clarkson's she couldn't help but flash an accusing and disappointed look in their direction.

Just as Shannon passed by the attorney tables she heard the sound of wood scraping on wood. She turned her head in the direction of the noise to find Lamar pushing his chair back from the table and before anyone could do anything, Lamar growled and lunged at her. He wrapped his hands around her neck and squeezed. His grip so tight it stifled her screams. Together they tumbled to the floor. As they fell, Shannon hit her left cheekbone on the railing behind the attorney tables. A sharp pain shot through her face, her head rang like church bells and colorful fireworks flashed in front of her eyes. She still couldn't force a scream, nor could she breathe.

Court security officers pried Lamar's hands loose from Shannon's neck and pulled him off her. Her lungs inflated with air, stinging just for a moment until the second rush of air passed through. She fixed her gaze on Lamar as he fought to break free from the security guards. One of the officers tased him causing him to drop to the floor and flop like a tuna fish out of water. Within seconds, they'd cuffed him and removed him from the courtroom.

Shannon managed to push herself up to her hands and knees and the children's attorney helped her to her feet. "Are you okay?"

Shannon glanced around the courtroom. Fireworks still flashed in her eyes.

"Can you hear me? Are you okay?" the attorney asked again as he kept his hand wrapped around the upper part of her arm to help steady her.

She placed her hand over her cheek and squeezed her eyes shut. She opened her eyes and looked at the attorney. "I guess I'm okay, but my cheek kind of hurts."

A few minutes later court proceedings resumed without Lamar in the room. Judge Matthews denied the Clarkson's request for custody of their children. Chandra burst into tears and looked toward Shannon. "This is your fault. You'll pay for this!"

Shannon simply turned away from Chandra and walked out of the courtroom on unsteady legs.

She made it to her office without shedding a single tear. She pulled out her chair and the second she sat down the tears began to flow. She placed her elbows on her desk and rested her head in her hands despite her throbbing cheek.

"Are you okay?" Anna asked as she passed through the office doorway and took a stance in front of Shannon's desk staring down at her. "Court security just called and told me what happened."

Shannon lifted her head and looked up at Anna. "I guess. Lamar grabbed me and we tumbled to the ground. I hit my cheek on the wood rail on the way down. It hurts, I'm sure it's just bruised."

"Maybe you should go get it checked out and make sure the bone isn't cracked or anything. It looks like it's already starting to swell."

Shannon lifted herself from her chair, walked over to the file cabinet and pulled out her purse. She fumbled through it until she found her compact mirror. She popped it open and assessed her cheek, touching it lightly with her forefinger.

* * * *

Spinelli slammed his phone receiver down and sprang out of his chair before the court security officer could finish telling him about Shannon's altercation in the courtroom with Lamar Clarkson. He raced up the stairwell taking two steps at a time. He needed to see her. He needed to make sure she was okay. His quick heavy footsteps drew glances from Shannon and Anna as he passed through the doorway of Shannon's office.

He flashed a quick glance at Anna as he passed by her, then he zoned in on Shannon. He stared down into her big emerald green eyes. The redness splattered throughout the whites of her eyes and the swelling already occurring on the left side of her face drew his undivided attention. His heart jumped into his throat at the sight of her, nearly causing him to choke.

Spinelli fought hard to control himself. He wanted nothing more than to beat the shit out of the bastard that did this to her. He sucked in a deep breath and willed his heart out of his throat and back into his chest. He slowed his rapid-paced breathing back to normal. With his eyes fixed on Shannon, he took another step toward her. He placed his fingers under her chin and slowly lifted it to get a better look at her face. He worked to find a calm voice. "I just heard what happened. Are you okay?"

"I'm fine. It's nothing, really."

Though she spoke casually, he could tell by the fury in her eyes she was mad as hell at the asshole that did this to her. And the slight shiver penetrating her body told him of the pain she endured.

He cupped her face in his hands. Her skin felt warm to the touch. He used his thumbs to swipe the damp tears from her cheeks and continued to stare into her gaze. No matter how hard he tried, he just couldn't seem to pull his eyes away from hers.

Shannon unlocked her gaze and took a quick short step back, pulling away from him. "I appreciate your coming up here and your concern, Detective, but I'm fine."

Spinelli took the hint and stepped back as well. He felt his heart crack in half as she spoke. His mind raced for something to do or say in response to her but nothing surfaced. Disbelief filled him. His exceptional ability to read people, an ability he'd prided himself on through the years, seemed to disappear around Shannon. Her words not a second ago brushed him off yet the intense look in her eyes seemed to tell a different story. He kept his gaze locked on her, searching for anything, any clue at all to tell him how to reach her in the way he wanted. This unfamiliar territory made him anxious. He tucked his sweaty hands into the pockets of his jeans and cleared his throat.

"Well, I'm glad you're okay. I'll be back up this afternoon then as planned."

He searched her eyes one more time before he spun on his heel, nodded at Anna, and went out the door.

* * * *

Shannon stared after Spinelli as he walked out of her office. Her heart raced and an odd sensation rippled through her stomach. In her entire life, she'd never seen such intensity in a man's stare and it frightened her. She didn't know why it scared her but it did. She was sure he was going to kiss her, right in front of Anna, and she wanted him to kiss her but then her mouth took over and blew him off. *What in the hell is wrong with me?*

She could feel Anna's eyes on her. She shifted her gaze toward her to find her staring intently at her. The corners of Anna's mouth twitched upward. "Jesus Christ he's good looking. I've never seen such dark eyes. And you, my dear, are holding out on me," Anna accused as she grabbed a folder from the desk and used it to fan herself.

"What?" Shannon asked.

Anna shook her head. "Don't 'what' me. You and Mr. Hottie there. What's going on?"

Shannon frowned. "Nothing, there's nothing going on, just work."

"Nice try but I'm not buying it. That look between you two was so intense the building could have fallen down around you and neither one of you would have noticed."

Shannon shook her head. "We work together, and that's all. I don't really think he's that into me and he's really not my type. Plus I just don't have the time right now."

Anna rolled her eyes and blew out a sigh. "Shannon, dear, Shannon, I know I shouldn't complain seeing as I'm your boss but you focus too much on work. As your friend, I'm telling you that you need to get out and play a little. Go dancing or go to a movie. Go out and have some fun for a change. That's what people your age do, they go out and have fun."

Anna pointed at the doorway. "And the hottie you just sent packing, the one that eyes you up as if you're his favorite kind of candy, is just what you need."

"Anna, really, him? You're kidding, right?"

"Yes him. I'll tell you right now, if I were twenty years younger and single I'd be stuck to him like smoke on bacon."

Chapter Fourteen

Spinelli parked his truck next to Shannon's vehicle and waited for her. He wanted to check on her and make sure she was okay from her unpleasant encounter in the courtroom with Clarkson. After he'd left her office earlier in the day he found himself unable to concentrate on anything else other than her. And even though she'd brushed him off, with her words and actions, the look in her eyes had been unmistakable. He knew she wanted him. He wondered why she fought it. It was no secret they'd gotten off to a rocky start, but he thought that things had somewhat come around.

Glancing in the direction of the building, Spinelli caught Anna's warm gaze as she walked toward him. She stopped and stood next to his door. He lowered his window. She gave him a wide smile. "Take it your waiting for Shannon?"

Spinelli searched her mischievous eyes. "I am."

"She'll be out in just a minute." Anna shifted her gaze from Spinelli toward the building and then back to him again. "Any plans for tonight?"

"Not sure yet."

"Hmm," Anna replied with a nod. He could nearly see the wheels turning in her head.

Anna leaned closer to the window. "She's got a weakness for Mexican food. She loves El Maya, the place right down the street from her apartment." Anna chuckled. "Order her a margarita and she might even loosen up a bit."

Spinelli smiled. "Thanks for the tip."

"Not a problem. Have a nice night."

He watched as Anna slid into the car two stalls down, cranked the engine, and drove out of sight. He liked her, and he knew she cared for Shannon.

Moments later Shannon surfaced in the parking lot. A puzzled look came over her face when she noticed him. She walked up to his door. "Is something wrong? Did you find Roland's killer?"

"No, nothing's wrong, and we've got nothing new on the case." God how he wished he would find the killer. He worried about Shannon and feared for her safety.

Shannon pulled her eyebrows together. "Then why are you here?"

She stared at him and waited out his hesitation. "I was hoping you'd join me for dinner."

She stood silent, and appeared to be debating her answer.

"Do you like Mexican? I know a great place not far from your apartment," Spinelli chimed before she could say "no" and shatter his heart.

"El Maya?"

"Yeah, you know of it?"

Shannon nodded.

"I'll follow you home then we'll drive over there together."

"Okay," she replied with a small degree of reluctance.

Spinelli followed Shannon to her place. He debated sending Anna a "thank you" card or perhaps a bouquet of flowers.

Shannon parked her car and then climbed into his truck. Minutes later, they were being seated at the restaurant. The hostess took their drink order. Spinelli ordered a beer as Shannon glanced over the drink list. "Do you like margaritas?" he asked, remembering what Anna had mentioned to him earlier.

Shannon smiled. "I love margaritas but it's a work night."

Was she for real, Spinelli wondered, so pure, so naive, and so innocent? God he had to have her. He'd never met anyone like her before. He couldn't help but smile at her. "I think just one would be alright."

She nodded and ordered the margarita.

Most of the dinner conversation revolved around the case. On occasion, Shannon would interject with some information about her parents and her sister's family. He envied her. She appeared to have grown up in a normal family environment, the kind where everyone loves each other, and cares for one another. He wondered what that would have felt like. Anna was right. The margarita seemed to loosen Shannon up a bit. He hung on her every word wanting to hear more about her life.

Spinelli glanced down at their empty plates, and then at his watch. He'd give anything if the clock would just slow down. He wanted more time with her. The waitress came by with the dessert tray, and though he didn't want any more to eat he ordered dessert in an effort to buy more time.

Shannon passed on dessert but took a bite of his. His stomach fluttered at the sight of her wrapping her beautiful mouth around his fork. A bit of chocolate clung to her bottom lip. He considered swiping it away with his tongue. He wondered how it would taste mixed with her flavor. She lifted her napkin to her mouth and rid her lip of the chocolate. *Damn.*

After milking his dessert for as long as he possibly could, he paid the bill and drove her home. He walked her to her doorway. She turned to face him. "I had a nice time. Thanks for dinner."

He scanned her eyes, and leaned in. Her breath hitched. She looked nervous. He reached up and swiped his fingers lightly across her bruised cheek. When he'd seen her earlier in the day her cheek was red, from her altercation with Clarkson, but now shades of purple, splashed with yellow, covered her normally pale cheek. "Does it hurt?"

"A little bit when I talk or smile. It's not too bad."

The thought of Clarkson's hands on her angered him. "That asshole's lucky he's in jail. If he hadn't been…" Spinelli caught himself and stopped speaking. He'd wanted this moment to be nice. He hoped he hadn't ruined it. Her soft sweet gaze remained on him. *Still good.*

He dipped his head and pressed his lips gently to her bruised cheekbone. She sighed and then tilted her head to the side giving him better access. Her cheek felt warm and soothing to his lips. He eased his kisses over to her mouth. Her incredible scrumptious lips met his. Though he wanted more, he worked to keep the kiss light. He worried that if he rushed her she'd back off. He figured her for a much slower pace than which he was accustomed.

It took every bit of strength he could find to end the kiss. He took a step back. Pulling his gaze from her proved even more difficult. It was as though she wouldn't release him. She ran her tongue across her lips. Did she do that on purpose? He decided if she did it a second time he would deem it intentional, and would kiss her again. But this time he would kiss her like he wanted to in the first place, deep and long. He would explore her lovely mouth, every ounce of it. He stared at her beautiful mouth, waiting. She stared back.

He knew he needed to end this. If he stayed another second he wouldn't be able to control himself. The depth of his desire for her scared him. He cleared his throat. "Good night, Shannon. I'll see you tomorrow morning."

He turned and took a step before she spoke. "Wait," the desperation in her voice was unmistakable.

He spun around. She stepped toward him, reached up, wrapped her arms around his neck, and pulled him toward her. She pressed her soft moist lips to his. Her lips parted, inviting him in. His tongue caressed hers, slow, and controlled at first, but not for long. She met his quickening pace. She wove her fingers through his hair. He clasped his hands around her waist and pulled her tight to his body. Shock, pleasure, and heat spread through him like wildfire. He kissed her deeper, harder, wetter, and longer. He explored every ounce of her mouth absorbing her sweet flavor. His heart raced. He slid his lips from her mouth to her jaw, to her neck. She tilted her head back. A soft groan escaped her lips. He whispered her name and all of a sudden, as if hearing the sound of her name slapped her back into reality she pulled herself from him and stepped back. She looked confused.

He stepped toward her, and she stepped back.

"Are you okay?" Spinelli asked.

She threw her hand over her mouth and shook her head.

"What's the matter?"

"I'm so sorry. I can't believe I did that."

Spinelli raised an eyebrow. "Did what, kissed me?"

"Yes," she whispered.

Spinelli went out on a limb. "Well if it's any consolation, I didn't mind," he teased, trying to lighten the moment.

"Damn margaritas."

He fought the urge to smile.

"Didn't you like the kiss?" Judging from her initial response to his kiss, he was confident it was safe to ask.

"That's not the point."

"So you did like it."

She shifted her eyes to her feet.

"Well?" he pressed.

She lifted her gaze and met his. Her chest rose as she sucked in a breath. "It doesn't matter if I did or didn't, it's not going to happen again."

He stared at her, speechless, convinced his ears had deceived him. They'd perhaps just shared the most intimate sensual kiss of his life. Was it possible she could kiss like that and not mean it? Was she afraid, and if so, afraid of what?

His mind raced for something to say. He came up empty. He inched toward her, and reached for her. She stopped him with her hand. "It's just not going to work. We're two very different people. I'm sorry," she stammered.

Spinelli stood in the hallway, dumfounded. In silence, he watched as she turned and entered her apartment, shutting the door behind her. *That's it.* A crater the size of the Grand Canyon filled his chest where his heart used to be.

* * * *

Shannon flopped down on her bed. What had she just done? She knew by the look in Spinelli's eyes she'd hurt him. She didn't mean to but she did. She felt sick.

Damn it. He's not the type of man she'd planned on falling in love with. They were two very different people and he was messing up her plan. Her brain told her it would never work, her heart argued the opposite.

Her chest tightened, squeezing the life out of her.

She pressed her fingers to her lips as she thought about his first kiss.

It was slow, tender, and sweet. The second kiss, the one in which she nearly threw herself at him, left her breathless and weak. His mouth was so hot, erotic as sin. Never in her life had she felt such desire, need, and passion in a kiss. His lips, his moist possessive lips, were firm, yet soft.

She ran her tongue through her mouth seeking out every last bit of his flavor. Odd, a man could taste so sweet, especially a man who hunts down killers for a living.

Chapter Fifteen

Spinelli taped the wire to Officer Miller's chest as he and Walker prepped Miller for his first undercover assignment. Miller, a fresh academy graduate and newcomer to the department landed himself the undercover position as an elf due to his young age and looks. Spinelli tasked Miller to pose as a college student just trying to earn a little extra cash over the holiday season, the same situation as the other elves.

"We're almost there. Is he ready?" Marsh yelled from the driver's seat of the black Chevy police issue van.

"Yeah, he's ready," Spinelli replied as he flashed a look of assurance in Miller's direction. He could easily see the kid was nervous.

Spinelli knew Walker and Marsh were of like mind. They all hoped Miller would click with the other elves and work his way into the card game so they could find out exactly what it was all about. Spinelli knew in his gut the card game at the Greek restaurant had something to do with the murders of Hudson and Reed.

Marsh manned the van and surveillance equipment while Spinelli and Walker moseyed about the mall near the Santa display so they could keep their eyes on Miller.

Spinelli watched as Miller made his entrance into the Santa display. The night's crew consisted of an older gentleman playing Santa and three young elves, including Miller. One elf assumed responsibility for crowd control, his job being to control the flow of traffic to Santa. Miller assumed photography duties, taking pictures of the children as they talked with Santa, and the remaining elf assumed the duty of exit strategies, helping the children find their way back to their parents.

The elves were so busy during the two hour period in which the Santa display was open they hardly exchanged a word between them. Spinelli had hoped for more of an exchange, maybe the locker room banter would pay off.

Miller walked with the elves to the locker room. Spinelli watched from a distance. Once in the locker room Spinelli could no longer see Miller but he captured their conversation through his earpiece. Miller made mention of the fact that he's coming up a little short for next semester's tuition, hence the reason he took the job at the mall. In an effort to get them to offer up details about the card game, Miller pointed out that he's looking for another means to make a little more cash, but the elves offered nothing.

The subject of conversation turned to women and the elves informed Miller about the awesome looking babe that sometimes plays Santa's helper. They described in intricate detail how Shannon looked in her short little red dress, giving particular attention to her pale cleavage.

Spinelli's fists clenched. He didn't like hearing the elves talk about her like she was some sort of female piece of meat to be used and discarded once they were done having their fun with her.

One of the elves let out a chuckle. "I really wouldn't mind tapping that. She looks all innocent like all the time. I bet she's still a virgin."

"Oh yeah, hot and tight," the other elf commented.

Spinelli nearly blew a gasket at the sound of those words and it took every bit of strength he could muster not to storm into the locker room and beat some manners into the elves.

Miller piped in, "What's the story? Have either of you asked her out?"

"Nah, she's hot and all but she's a little older and I can't really picture her partying and having fun. She's probably one of those homebodies with four cats or something. I'm guessing she plays scrabble and drinks tea."

"But what if she's not like that at all?" Miller asked. "You could be missing out."

The elf thought for a moment, "Nah, I'm pretty sure she's all pure and innocent like. Plus it's no use anyhow. I think she might be going out with that older guy who plays Santa on the weekends."

"What makes you think that?"

"She was like waiting for him to come out of the locker room the other night and then they left together. You gotta wonder why she'd go after a loser like that."

"What's with the Santa guy? Why's he a loser?" Miller couldn't help but ask.

"Well, he's like, I don't know, at least in his thirties and he's working as Santa," the elf replied. "What the hell, can't he get a real job? And he's the worst Santa I've ever seen. It's like the kids scare the hell out of him or something."

Marsh and Walker roared with laughter as the elf rambled on and on about what a loser Spinelli was. Spinelli, hearing it all through his earpiece, did not see the humor.

Spinelli lurked behind a marble pillar as Miller and the elves left the locker room.

"Hey, you guys want to go get a beer?" Miller asked.

He watched the elves and waited for their response. The elves looked at each other for a moment and then back at Miller. "We can't. We've got a biology final at eight tomorrow morning," the taller of the two elves replied.

"Oh, okay. Maybe next time," Miller replied as he broke away from the elves and headed toward the parking ramp.

Spinelli continued to tail the elves. Just like the night before they walked up to the security gate at the Greek restaurant and Loukas the Greek's muscleman opened the gate and let the elves pass through.

Spinelli entered the van. "Well that didn't work. Something's going on in that restaurant and we need to find out what it is. We'll try this approach again tomorrow night."

Spinelli couldn't help but notice the shit-eating grins on Walker, Marsh and Miller's faces. "What? What's so funny?"

"Just you. You 'loser' old man. And what's this? The mighty Spinelli is afraid of a bunch of four-year-olds," Walker teased before his uncontrollable laughter echoed throughout the van. Marsh and Millers laughter chorused Walker's.

Spinelli flashed a hard-eyed scowl at Miller. He figured with him being new and all he could somewhat intimidate him. It worked and he stopped laughing.

"So, I'm going to work undercover again tomorrow night?" Miller asked.

"Yes," Spinelli replied.

Miller's eyes lit up. "Great, I hope to hell this Shannon chick is working tomorrow. Christ the way the guys were talking she must be freaking hot."

Spinelli's hard-eyed scowl at Miller grew harder. He pointed his finger in Miller's face. "Listen here, you're not here to pick up chicks. This is not fun and games. There have been two murders, two lives taken. Furthermore, she is not a chick. Show a little respect."

Walker leaned between Spinelli and Miller causing Spinelli to unlatch his glare on Miller. "Hey, the kid didn't know."

Miller's eyes were as wide as fifty-cent pieces. He cut his glance from Spinelli to Walker.

Walker glanced at Miller. "He's just a little protective of Shannon."

Miller shifted his eyes back to Spinelli. "Sorry."

"Can we just go? Marsh, get us the hell out of here," Spinelli snapped.

Chapter Sixteen

Spinelli found himself in an unusual situation, home alone on a Friday night watching ESPN while drinking beer and eating pizza. He couldn't remember the last time he spent a Friday night alone. In fact, he couldn't recall it ever happening before. On a typical Friday night, he would be out enjoying the company of someone of the opposite sex, or shooting pool with his buddies at the very least. But none of that seemed to interest him tonight.

As he took a swig of his beer, he pondered the events of the past week. His mind drifted to the Santa and elf murder case. No breaks yet. His mind wandered to thoughts of Shannon and he drew another swig of beer. No breaks there either. She'd been avoiding him since their date the other night. He'd left her three messages in the past day and a half, all unreturned. *Damn it.* Spinelli lifted his beer bottle to his lips again. *Why can't I break through her force field? What is it? Burned? Lesbian? No, can't be, I know she wants me, I can see it in her eyes and I can feel it when I touch her. And that kiss the other night, that mind boggling kiss. There's no way she faked that kind of passion. Damn it.*

Spinelli drained the bottle and then rested his head against the back of the chair and closed his eyes. He fantasized about Shannon in her little red velvet Santa helper dress. In his daydream, he kissed her in a deep possessive manner, his tongue dancing with hers. Her sweet flavor matched that of her sweet scent. He pulled his lips from hers and skimmed them over her chin, down her neck, and onto her chest. His intensified breathing caused the furry white trim of her dress to flutter about on the small portion of her exposed breasts. He continued to shower her neck and chest with kisses. He used his fingers to trace along the edge of the soft white trim of her dress. He began lowering his hand with every intention of plunging it between her dress and skin to cup her breast but before he was able to do so a loud rapid knock on his front door interrupted his fantasy.

Under protest Spinelli shook the fantasy from his head and glanced at his watch, 10:00 p.m. "Who in the hell is knocking on my door this late," he said out loud.

He lifted himself from his chair, walked over to the front door, and opened it. The second he opened the door Shannon sprang through the doorway as quick as a jack-in-the-box. She threw her arms around his waist, pulled herself tightly to his body, and sobbed into his chest.

Instinctively Spinelli wrapped his arms around her and visually scanned the immediate neighborhood. Seeing no unusual activity, he pushed the door shut and locked it.

With one arm wrapped tightly around her waist, Spinelli lifted his other arm and softly rubbed her back. He rested his chin lightly against the side of her head, her soft hair brushing against his cheek. He breathed in her scent. She always wore the same sexy scent. It reminded him of a fresh spring morning.

Shannon continued to cry and breathe erratically.

He brushed his lips lightly on the top of her head. "Shh, Sweetheart, it's okay."

God how he wanted her to stop crying. He couldn't take her being upset. He still didn't know what upset her but whatever the reason he felt a compelling need to fix it.

Her sobs began to subside and her breathing became more controlled.

Spinelli loosened his hold and inched back a bit. He looked down at her. She lifted her head and looked up at him with her big emerald green eyes. He could see the fear in them. He cupped her head in his hands and ran his thumbs across her cheeks to swipe the moisture away.

"Do you want to tell me what happened, Sweetheart?"

* * * *

81

Shannon nodded and inhaled deeply, "I parked my car on the second floor of the parking ramp at the mall. I needed to pick up the donated toys from the drop box by the Santa display, for the church. Anyhow, I got out of my car and headed toward the elevator. The elevator doors opened so I looked in and saw one of the guys that work at the Greek restaurant, you know, one of the guys always standing by the entryway to the restaurant at closing time."

Shannon paused. She chewed on her lips for a moment. Tears flooded her eyes. Spinelli reached forward and took her hands in his. "What happened, Sweetheart? What was he doing?"

Shannon released her lips. "He had..." Her voice cracked and she paused again. She closed her eyes and gathered her thoughts. She opened her eyes to find Spinelli's gaze still fixed on her. His warm caring eyes eased her and she continued, "He had a body slung over his shoulder and he threw it out of the elevator. It startled me. I jumped back and dropped my keys on the cement floor. The noise drew his attention and he looked at me. Judging from the look on his face, he seemed surprised to see me but then the look turned stone cold. I felt frozen. I couldn't move. He lunged toward me but the elevator doors shut him inside. I glanced down at the body and realized it was Jarrod, you know, one of the elves. He was moaning. I didn't know what to do. I was afraid the guy in the elevator was going to come back so I got back into my car and took off. When I got out of the parking ramp I called 911 for Jarrod and then I drove here."

* * * *

Spinelli ran to his front window and peeked through the blinds. He turned back toward Shannon. "Did you notice if anyone followed you here?"

Shannon used the back of her hand to swipe the tears from her cheek. "I don't think so. It all happened so fast. I didn't know what to do." She burst into tears again.

He reached for her and pulled her tightly to him. His mind raced. He wondered if Loukas the Greek's muscleman recognized her. He feared for her safety.

Shannon stopped crying and Spinelli separated himself from her. He motioned for her to take a seat on his couch. He punched Walker's number on his cell phone and when he answered, Spinelli gave him an overview of the events of Shannon's evening.

Spinelli snapped his phone shut and took a seat next to Shannon on the couch. He reached over, took her small trembling hands into his, and looked into her frightened eyes. "Are you okay? Can I get you anything?"

"I'm fine. I'm just worried about Jarrod."

"Walker's going to check on Jarrod. But for now I need you to tell me every detail again. What exactly did you see and hear and more importantly do you think the guy in the elevator knows who you are?"

Shannon sniffled again and then she took in a deep breath and let it out slowly.

Spinelli listened as she repeated the story reiterating and adding every detail she could remember.

"Do you think he recognized you?" Spinelli asked again.

Shannon blinked away the tears in her eyes. "I don't know. It all happened so fast."

"Are you positive it was one of Loukas' guys in the elevator?"

Shannon hesitated and thought for a moment. "I'm pretty sure it was but it was dark."

"Would you recognize him if you saw him again?"

"I think so."

Spinelli nodded. He wished she wasn't quite so indecisive about whether or not the man in the elevator was one of Loukas' men.

Just as Shannon finished her rendition Spinelli's cell phone rang. Walker reported that he located Jarrod, alive, at County Hospital, but he didn't have any other details yet.

Spinelli rose from the couch pulling Shannon up with him. "I need to go to the hospital and talk with Jarrod, see if he can tell me what happened and why."

Shannon watched him as he flung his black leather jacket over his shoulders. "Oh...I guess I'll go home then. Please let me know how Jarrod is doing when you find out."

Spinelli zipped his jacket and narrowed the gap between them. He couldn't believe what she just said. She couldn't possibly be that naive?

She obviously didn't comprehend the degree of danger surrounding her. He placed his hand on her shoulder and caught her gaze. "I don't think it's a good idea for you to be alone right now. If Loukas the Greek's sidekick recognized you...you know what, until I figure out what's going on here I think maybe it would be a good idea if you just hung with me. Okay?"

Shannon blew out a sigh and nodded. Spinelli grabbed her hand and led her through the house to the door to the garage. He helped her into the truck, then hurried around to the driver's side.

Spinelli drove to the hospital and listened to Shannon as she repeated the details of the incident over and over. When they got to the hospital, she repeated her story to both Walker and Marsh as they waited for word from the ER doctor about Jarrod.

Finally, the short portly ER doctor came into the small waiting room to give an update on Jarrod's status. He looked at Walker and Marsh. "The young man's been roughed up pretty good." Then the doctor looked at Spinelli. "He's got a few cracked ribs, a gash on his forehead which required nine stitches, and a great deal of bruising on his face and abdomen." The doctor held up his pudgy hand for everyone to see and he pointed at a couple of areas on the base of his hand as he spoke. "The boy also has several broken bones in his left hand. Here, here and right here." The doctor lowered his hand and glanced in the direction of Jarrod's room.

"Can we talk to him now?" Spinelli asked the ER doctor.

The doctor held up his hand and raised two fingers. "Yes. You can talk to him. Two minutes, that's it. The boy needs his rest."

They entered Jarrod's room and Spinelli went to one side of the bed, and Marsh and Walker lined up on the other side. Shannon stood just inside the doorway watching from a distance.

Spinelli leaned slightly over Jarrod's bed. "Jarrod, can you hear me?"

Jarrod's eyes popped open, the swollen eye not quite as open as the other eye. He shifted his eyes around taking in the sight of the three men staring down at him. When his eyes made the full circle and returned to Spinelli he took a double-take and pulled his eyebrows together. "Santa."

"Well, actually, Detective Spinelli."

"That explains a few things," Jarrod muttered as he winced.

"What do you mean?" Spinelli asked thinking the response must pertain to something to do with Jarrod's assault.

"You suck as Santa," Jarrod flippantly replied.

Walker and Marsh chuckled. Spinelli cut them a sharp look. He didn't like being poked fun at and he didn't like not being good at something. He'd grown accustom to being good at whatever he did.

Spinelli loosened his hard-eyed scowl. "Can we just stick to the issue at hand here?"

Spinelli turned his attention back to Jarrod who drifted in and out of sleep as they questioned him. Jarrod offered nothing. He claimed he couldn't remember anything between the time he left the locker room and the time he woke up in the hospital.

A short time later, a nurse came into Jarrod's room and shooed them out. As they walked down the hall and toward the parking lot Shannon listened attentively as the detectives talked about their next step and the fact that Jarrod just lied to them. They knew Jarrod held his tongue solely out of fear.

A plain-clothes officer was posted outside Jarrod's room for protection. Spinelli, Walker, and Marsh decided not to pick up Loukas the Greek's muscleman just yet. They decided to tail him instead, along with Tyler Simmons, the other elf.

Chapter Seventeen

Spinelli turned out of the hospital parking lot and headed in the direction of Shannon's apartment. She sat quietly in the passenger seat. Out of the corner of his eye, he could see her tilt her head to the side. A puzzled look consumed her face and she opened her mouth, "Ah, I need my car. It's at your house."

Spinelli cringed inside. He hoped she wouldn't give him any flack about staying at his place. Thoughts of Loukas the Greek's muscleman paying her a visit scared the hell out of him. For her own safety he didn't want her to stay at her apartment.

He cleared his throat. "I thought we agreed that you'd just hang with me for a while so I thought we'd stop by your place so you could get some things and then we'd go back to my place."

Spinelli paused, took a half breath, and continued talking about the incident at the mall so that Shannon could not get a protesting word in edgewise. He saw her open her mouth a couple of times but he just kept talking and before he knew it, he'd parked his truck in her apartment complex's parking lot.

"Well we're here," Spinelli said as he sprang out of the truck and hurried to the passenger side of the vehicle to open the door for her.

Shannon slid out of the truck and slung her handbag over her shoulder. Spinelli walked beside her as she headed toward the front door of her apartment building. He combed the area looking for anything unusual. The apartment complex appeared dark and quiet.

Shannon punched the pass code into the numeric keypad, the door buzzed and Spinelli pushed it open. He held the door open for her to pass through then he followed her down the long narrow hallway. She glanced over her shoulder at him. "Do you really think this is necessary?"

Spinelli cocked his head to the side. "What do you mean?"

"That I can't stay here, that I need to stay at your place."

Spinelli opened his mouth, ready to go into detail about his concern for her well-being but before any sound could escape Mrs. Finch's apartment door opened and she popped her head into the hallway. "Is that you, dear?"

"Yes. Wow you're up kind of late tonight."

Mrs. Finch let out a frail chuckle. "It is kind of late but Sister and I got caught up in the Golden Girls marathon on TV. That Estelle Getty, she's a firecracker that one, I just love to listen to her."

Spinelli couldn't help but smile and tease Mrs. Finch. "Estelle kind of reminds me of you. I think you're a little firecracker yourself."

His assessment brought a wide smile to Mrs. Finch's face. She stepped toward him and reached up with her cold frail boney hand and placed it on his cheek and gave it a little pat. "Oh you're a charmer."

Mrs. Finch lowered her hand, looked in Shannon's direction, and flashed a little wink. "I think he's a keeper, dear, much more personable than the caller that came by for you earlier tonight."

A blanket of jealousy fell over Spinelli. "She had a caller did she? Is this someone I need to worry about Mrs. Finch?"

Before the words even finished coming out of his mouth he could feel Shannon's glare on him.

Mrs. Finch leaned toward Spinelli and whispered, "I wouldn't worry about it. This fella didn't seem very nice. Shannon here, she likes the nice ones." Mrs. Finch let out a chuckle and continued in her loud whisper. "You smell better too."

Spinelli caught Shannon's eye-roll and he could tell she was nearly bursting at the seams to find out who her visitor was.

"Mrs. Finch, what time was my visitor here and did he mention his name or what he wanted?"

"He came by at about 11:00. I heard someone in the hallway so I opened the door thinking it would be you and as soon as I caught a whiff of him, I knew it wasn't you. I asked if I could help him and he said you were expecting him. I told him you weren't home yet and he said he would wait around for a bit. He wasn't much of a talker."

Spinelli immediately thought the worst. Loukas the Greek's muscleman already came by looking for her.

"Mrs. Finch, did your sister get a look at Shannon's visitor?" Spinelli asked hoping to get a good description.

Mrs. Finch shook her head. "No, she didn't come to the door at all. Like I said he wasn't much of a talker so the whole conversation didn't take but a minute."

A rush of disappointment rippled through Spinelli. "Are there any attributes you can describe about him for me?"

Mrs. Finch perched her hands on her narrow hips. "Well, he's got a big shadow, not only tall but wide. And he's got a deep mono-tone voice and he breathes kind of heavy. He smelled like fresh baked bread and garlic. He made me hungry."

Spinelli thanked Mrs. Finch for her time, wished her a good night, and followed Shannon into her apartment.

Shannon hung her handbag on the coat tree next to the door. She turned and looked up at Spinelli. "It was him, wasn't it?"

He knew she knew but apparently she needed to hear him say out loud, "Yeah, pretty sure."

Shannon nodded. "I'll get my things." And she spun on her heel and headed down the short hallway toward her bedroom.

Spinelli snooped about Shannon's apartment as he waited for her. He eyed her basic beige furniture and immediately concluded that it suited her conservative nature. He liked her lightly decorated living room walls, a picture hung here or there but none of that cluttered looking home decorators stuff covered her walls. A wood shelving unit stood in the corner of the living room. Two of the shelves where lined with romance novels and the other two shelves housed pictures of people. The largest picture on the shelf looked like a family photo. It consisted of a woman who looked a lot like Shannon but a bit older and a lawyer looking gentleman a bit older than the woman in the photo. Three little red-headed boys with freckles stood in front of the couple.

"That's my sister, Claire and her family, her husband John and their boys, Cody, Zack, and Brady. They live in Boston now. I don't get to see them much since they moved away," Shannon said as she lifted the photo from the shelf and pulled it closer to her sad eyes.

Spinelli grabbed the duffel bag from her hand. "Got everything?"

She flashed her eyes around her living room and then nodded.

Silence filled the air during the ride back to Spinelli's house. He could easily see the worry lines take over Shannon's milky white face. His heart felt heavy. What he would give to take her worry away.

Shannon followed Spinelli into his house, through the kitchen and into the small hallway which opened the way to two bedrooms, a small office, and a bathroom. He stopped in the middle of the hallway and pointed to his right. "That's my bedroom at the end of the hall and then there's my office."

He resumed walking in the opposite direction of his bedroom. He opened another door. "Here's the bathroom," he said as he continued walking, "and here's the spare bedroom."

He pushed his way through the doorway and set her duffel bag on the bed. He looked around the room and then fixed his gaze on her. "Think you'll be okay in here?" he asked, hoping she'd say no and ask to share his room.

Shannon nodded. She wasn't much for talking the past several hours.

Spinelli glanced down at his watch. "Wow, its 2:00 a.m. already. You must be exhausted."

She nodded again.

"I'll get out of here so you can get some rest. I'll be just down the hall if you need anything."

He got the same response. A nod.

Spinelli left Shannon alone in the spare bedroom, closing the door behind him as he left. He made sure to lock both the front and back door. He peeked through the living room blinds and stared out onto the street in front of his house looking for anything out of the ordinary. A hint of unease coiled around his chest at the thought of Loukas the Greek's muscleman paying her a visit. He double-checked the front and back doors, making sure they were locked.

He glanced through the blinds once again then he straightened them out and turned off the lights in the living room and kitchen. He stepped into the hallway and glanced to his left. He could see the light still shining under Shannon's bedroom door. He turned and headed toward his bedroom.

Spinelli pulled his Beretta 9mm from his holster and tucked it into the drawer of his nightstand along with his badge. He pulled his shirt over his head as he walked toward the master bathroom and flung it over the bedpost. He unbuttoned his jeans and kicked them off along the way as well.

He couldn't wait to climb into bed, he felt dead tired. As he brushed and flossed his teeth he thought about Jarrod's apprehension as he and Walker and Marsh questioned him. He recalled how Jarrod intentionally seemed to avoid looking him in the eye as he spoke with him and how his left eye twitched uncontrollably. Deep down he knew whatever or whoever Jarrod was involved with scared him. The questions still remained, who's involved and what's it about?

Spinelli flung the covers back on his bed and climbed between the crisp cool sheets. They felt good against his weary skin. He pulled the covers up around his neck and rolled onto his left side. He lay there staring at the backside of the door leading to the hallway. Spinelli wondered if Shannon was asleep, he speculated about what she wore when she slept, and he fantasized about what they would be doing if she were in his bed right now. He visualized her naked, her soft smooth silky white skin touching his. He imagined cupping her small round breasts in his hands and teasing her nipples with his thumb and forefinger, and then perhaps his mouth, he grew hot and hard at the thought. He envisioned entering her, knowing she would be soft as velvet. His fantasy felt so vivid he actually felt her warmth surrounding him.

Eventually Spinelli cleared his mind enough to drift off to sleep and he slept uninterrupted until he heard the shower running in his spare bathroom. He forced his still weary eyes open and glanced at the clock. "8:00 a.m. What is she doing up so early?" he whispered.

He blew out a sigh, flung the covers back, and swung his tired legs over the side of the bed. He sat there thinking that he could really use a couple more hours of sleep, five to six hours just didn't cut it for him. He forced himself off the bed and put on a pair of jeans. Barefoot and shirtless he wandered to the kitchen to make a pot of coffee. Needing a kick-start he dumped four heaping scoops of coffee grounds into the filter rather than the usual three. The shower still ran.

Spinelli wandered into his office and logged onto his computer, his normal Saturday routine. First things first, he would check his usual sports websites, then take in a little local and national news, and when fully awake he would do a little research on Loukas the Greek.

As the computer booted up he walked back to the kitchen to get a cup of coffee. The shower still ran. He leaned against the kitchen counter and sipped on his coffee. He glanced up at the clock. It read 8:20. He knew from experience that his old water heater didn't allow for a hot twenty minute shower. He'd been meaning to get a new water heater but hadn't checked it off his list yet.

A few more minutes passed and the shower still ran. A wave of concern rippled throughout his body. He set his coffee cup on the kitchen countertop and walked over to the bathroom door. Pressing his ear to the door, he could only hear the shower running. He knocked on the door but Shannon didn't respond. His heart began to race. He debated barging into the bathroom to check on her. He knocked on the door again, and again no response. "Shannon, are you okay?" he asked, still no response.

He opened the door and glanced in the direction of the tub to find the shower curtain pulled shut. "Shannon, are you okay? If you don't answer I'm going to open the curtain."

Hearing no response, he flung the shower curtain back to find her sitting in the tub with her knees pulled to her chest and arms wrapped tightly around them. She'd pressed her face against the top of her knees and her long curly wet red hair clung to her legs and back.

Spinelli reached into the shower and shut off the freezing cold water. The water stopped pelting her shivering body. He grabbed a towel and flung it over her shoulders. He used his hands to rub her shoulders and arms in an effort to warm her then he wrapped his hands around the upper part of her arms and lifted upward, but she didn't budge. "Come on Sweetheart, let's get you out of here, and warm you up."

Shannon lifted her head and looked at him. His heart nearly stopped at the sight of her red-stained eyes. He shifted his gaze from her eyes to her lips, which displayed the bluest color he'd ever seen on a person. He edged one of his arms under her knees and the other under her arms and lifted her cold wet body out of the tub. He carried her to his bedroom. He sat down on the edge of his bed with her on his lap and he pulled the heavy quilt from the bed and wrapped it around them.

She rested her head on his shoulder and buried her face in the crook of his neck. He rubbed her arms, hands, and feet in an attempt to warm them. Her toes felt cold as ice cubes. After a few minutes, he could feel her frigid body start to warm and her shivering stopped.

Spinelli lifted his hand and stroked her damp hair. "It's okay, Sweetheart. Everything will be okay."

Shannon lifted her head and looked at him. "No it won't, that's just it. They won't let it end. I know these kinds of people. I see it every day at work. They won't stop until they get what they want."

"Who and what are you talking about?"

"I don't know who for sure. I can only assume it's the guy I saw in the elevator with Jarrod who called me."

"Someone called you, when?"

"This morning on my cell. The call woke me up."

"What did he say?" Spinelli asked in a voice a bit more frantic than he'd wished.

Shannon chewed on her lower lip for a moment. Her eyes flooded with tears.

Spinelli calmed and softened his voice. "Sweetheart, I need to know what he said."

Shannon released her lips from her teeth. "He said as long as I keep my mouth shut no one around me will get hurt, including the three little red-headed boys in the photo on my bookshelf."

She paused and sucked her lips back into her mouth. Waves of tears fell from her eyes and rolled down her cheeks.

"Is there more?"

Shannon nodded and used the back of her hand to clear the tears from her cheeks then she released her lips from her teeth again. "He said that if I go to the police I've seen my nephews for the last time."

Spinelli tightened his grip on her and held her until she stopped crying. He pressed his lips lightly to the top of her head then he scooted her off his lap and rose to his feet. "Why don't you lie down and get some more rest."

"No, I'm okay. What are you going to do?" she asked as she placed the palms of her hands on the bed and started to lift herself up.

Spinelli quickly rested his hand on her shoulder to ease her down. He squatted down and lifted her legs onto the bed, gently forcing her to lie down. He knelt next to the bed, reached up, and snugged the quilt around her neck. She looked like a curled up mummy all snuggly wrapped.

"You rest. I'm going to call Walker and Marsh and we're going to figure this out," Spinelli said and then he leaned over and pressed his lips lightly to her forehead. On his way out of the bedroom, he grabbed a T-shirt and flung it over his head.

Chapter Eighteen

While Shannon rested, Spinelli, Walker and Marsh discussed their game plan. The plan was almost completely in order before Spinelli heard Shannon stirring about in the hall. Then her cell phone rang. He and the other two fixed their eyes on the phone on the kitchen countertop. He reached for the phone but Shannon appeared between him and Walker and snatched it up. She looked at the display and then looked at Spinelli. "It's just Anna."

"Oh, okay," he replied as if giving her permission to answer the call.

"Hi Anna...I'm sorry I forgot we planned on going. Can you hold on a second?" Shannon glanced at the three of them. "I'm just going to take this in the other room."

Spinelli nodded and she walked away. He stared after her. The sight of her wearing his red plaid robe caused his sexual juices to flow and beg for release.

"Christ, she's freaking hot when she's not wearing those drab business suits," Marsh commented as he stared after her with the look of a starving wolf.

Spinelli's jealousy took over and he stepped into Marsh's sightline to block his view of her. Spinelli opened his mouth to speak but before a word could be released, Walker quickly stepped between Spinelli and Marsh. "Let's go Marsh. We've got work to do."

Walker and Marsh left and Spinelli went into his office to do a little internet research on Loukas the Greek. The thin walls of his old house allowed him to hear part of Shannon's phone conversation. Hearing his name roll off her tongue sparked his interest so he stepped lightly over to the doorway of his office so he could hear her better. The hallway acoustics allowed him to hear nearly every word exchanged between Shannon and Anna.

"Your voice sounds like its echoing. Did you flip me on speaker?" Anna asked.

"Yeah, I'm changing."

"What?"

"I'm changing."

"I thought you weren't home," Anna replied.

Spinelli waited out the long pause that followed Anna's reply. He wondered how sweet little naïve Shannon would respond.

As if a light bulb came on within her Anna ended the silence. "My God, you're at his house aren't you? Hot damn, it's about freaking time."

"No, it's not what you think. I'm not, we didn't," Shannon mumbled before Anna piped in again.

"Hey, you don't need to lie to me. You're an adult. For God's sake it's okay to have some fun. And come on, throw the old lady a bone here, just tell me one thing—is he as good as he looks?" Anna asked as she let out a girlish giggle.

Spinelli continued to listen for Shannon's response. He knew he shouldn't eavesdrop but he just couldn't help himself. And much to his surprise her tongue loosened.

"Okay, okay, if you must know, honestly I did not sleep with him."

"But you spent the night," Anna interjected.

Shannon snapped back, "Hey, if you want details don't interrupt me."

"Okay, sorry."

"It's a long story but we didn't have sex. Though I must admit when I saw him this morning wearing just a pair of jeans and no shirt it took about every piece of strength I could muster not to jump his bones right then and there. What he did for that pair of jeans should be illegal."

"Christ, I can imagine," Anna cut in.

"Hey, stop interrupting."

"Sorry."

"Anyhow, you should see him without a shirt on, my God, I just wanted to take my hands, and rub them over his washboard ripples they looked so firm and inviting. And when he looks at me with those dark charcoal eyes I nearly melt right there on the spot. Every intelligent thought in my head disappears and all I can think about is him taking me. I've never wanted, no needed, a man so bad in my life. It actually hurts."

Spinelli stood in the hallway dumfounded and hard as a rock. An urgency for release flowed through him. He debated crashing through her bedroom door and taking her right where she stood.

Anna's voice interrupted his thoughts. "Shannon, why on earth are you on the phone telling me about this rather than in his bed?"

"Well, I don't want him to think I'm a slut or something. We hardly know each other, and what if he doesn't feel as strongly for me as I do for him?"

Anna chuckled. "Where do you come from? Don't tell me you haven't noticed how he looks at you. And for God's sake you're the furthest thing from a slut I've ever seen. When was the last time you had sex?"

Spinelli continued to listen, nearly bursting at the seams.

"When?" Anna pressed.

Shannon blew out a sigh. "It's been so long I don't really remember."

"Shannon, you need to hang up this phone right now and go to him," Anna said firmly and she disconnected the call so quickly once she made her demand Spinelli was sure it was so Shannon could not reply to her.

"Thank you Anna Fontaine," Spinelli whispered to himself.

Spinelli saw the door to Shannon's room begin to open so he quickly retreated, back into his office and took a seat on his office chair. He faced the computer and began to click through some websites involving organized crime. Within seconds, he could feel the warmth of her body behind him. She leaned forward and looked at the computer screen, her soft milky white cheek just centimeters from his cheek.

Spinelli flashed his eyes toward the clock on the bottom right-hand corner of his computer monitor. The time read 3:30. Their shift at the mall didn't start until 5:00. He wished for more time.

In one swift movement, he spun in his chair and swept her onto his lap. Her green eyes widened but she didn't resist. He leaned his head forward and brushed his lips lightly across hers. His heart leaped into his throat. He hadn't fully expected the incalculable depth of intensity that swept through his veins the second her soft moist lips touched his. He needed a second. He pulled his head back and looked at her, his stomach trembled. Never in his life had a woman had such an effect on him. He could hardly breathe and he hadn't really even touched her yet. Her beauty mesmerized him. Her eyes darkened. She leaned forward and pressed her plump sweet lips to his again. She wrapped her arms around him and bound him closer. Her fingers wove through his hair. Every nerve ending in his body tingled and a rush of urgency flowed through him.

Slowly, he demanded himself, but the intensity of her touch nearly drove him insane. He met her demand for more pulling her body even tighter to his. She parted her lips slightly to let his tongue pass through. He caressed her tongue with his, tasting her sweet flavor. His head spun and he fought for control, but lost. Raw need spurted through him at the speed of sound. He feasted on her mouth as if there were going to be no tomorrow.

Shannon's breath hitched and she pulled away from him and lifted herself from his lap. She stood before him wearing her soft short red velvet Santa helper outfit. Was that it, as far as this was going? Did his untamed urgency scare her? Desire and need filled him. He'd had a taste of her and desperately needed more. Her mouth, not a second ago cried for more. He slowly scanned her from top to bottom with his hungry eyes. He wondered what she wore under that sexy dress. He wondered if her bra and panties matched her conservative nature he'd often witnessed at work or if they validated the way he saw her in that sexy red dress.

Spinelli looked up and caught her gaze. Her eyes spoke to him, telling him she wanted more. He leaned forward in his chair and placed his right hand slightly above and to the side of her left knee. Without breaking his gaze, he began to slowly slide his hand up her leg and under her dress. The furry white trim of her dress tickled his forearm. His hand paused at the top of her thigh-high silk stocking. His breath caught. Never did he imagine that her conservative nature would allow her to wear something so sexy. He figured her for a full pantyhose gal. He couldn't help wonder what other surprises she held. The desire to know what kind of panties covered her sweet treasure unleashed the rabid beast within him again. He fought the beast, tucking the urgency aside. He wanted to take it slowly and savor every second of being with her, but her shear sexiness made it difficult.

Still with his gaze fixed on her he reached up with his other hand and slid it up her leg until it too rested at the top of her thigh-high silk stocking. He used his thumbs to flip the edge of her stocking over and began rolling it downward. She placed her hands on his shoulders for support, bent her knee, and lifted her leg so he could roll the stocking all the way down and completely off her foot. He tossed the stocking aside and reached for the other one using the same slow pace. He tossed that stocking aside.

He quickened his pace just a bit as he reached up under her dress to quench his curiosity. His fingers tingled as he skimmed them over her soft smooth skin. His breath caught at the feel of the small patch of silky material that rested between his hand and heaven. His blood pounded in his ears.

Shannon widened her stance and instinctively he placed his hand on her lower abdomen and gently slid it under the thin waistband of her panties. He caressed her with his fingers as he slid her skimpy red silk panties off her.

He plunged his finger into her soft swollen wetness. Her breath hitched and she tightened her grip on his shoulders. He watched her as her eyes began to glaze over. She placed her hand over his and gave it a slight squeeze. She tore her gaze from his and flashed her eyes in the direction of his bedroom. "Nick, I want you in me."

The sound of his name rolling off her sweet tongue nearly drove him insane. Not once since they met did she call him by his first name. She always referred to him as Detective or Detective Spinelli, never Nick. In his mind, he begged her to say it again and almost as if she'd heard him she leaned forward placing her mouth to his ear and whispered, "Come with me, Nick."

She gave his hand a slight tug and he rose from his chair, and followed her to his bedroom. She tugged at his shirt and slid her hands under it. She caressed his stomach. The feel of her small soft hands on his stomach felt like gold. His urgency grew. He pulled his shirt over his head and kicked off his jeans. He reached toward her and pulled her dress up over her head giving him a first-hand glance at her small partially covered round pale-skinned breasts. With one quick smooth motion of his thumb and forefinger, he undid the small single clasp that held her bra on and her breasts in place. The second the clasp came undone her perky breasts pushed the silky red material off to the sides and bounced slightly. He could hear her taut nipples begging for his mouth.

Shannon stepped backwards until the back of her legs found the bed then she lowered herself onto it and scooted over to make room for him. Her hair spilled like fire over the pillow. He scanned her naked body.

"God, you're beautiful."

He crawled in beside her and lay next to her leaning up on one elbow gazing deeply into the sea of green that stared back at him. Desire filled them.

He leaned toward her and skimmed his mouth over hers. Then he took her mouth swallowing her soft sigh. He slowly stroked her smooth flat stomach with his hand while his lips trailed down to her neck. He slid his hand up and cupped her small breast. It fit so perfectly into his palm it nearly undid him. Unable to resist, he lowered his kisses down from her neck to her chest and then to her breasts. He needed a taste. He massaged her taut nipples with his tongue, giving each one their due attention. His hand drifted lower. He found her wet, swollen and ready for him. He pressed his hand to her wetness. She gasped and let out a deep, throaty moan, music to his ears. His own pleasure grew from hers and the movements of her body told him she was ready for him.

Spinelli reached back toward his nightstand and opened the drawer. He retrieved a condom. Shannon sat up and took the small square package from his hand, opened it and slid the condom on him. Her small hands sheathing him was the most erotic experience. His heart nearly leaped out of his chest. His body begged for release.

Shannon eased her body down. Spinelli gazed into her eyes as he positioned his body on top of hers then he gently slid himself inside her. He stroked slow and deep, and she felt just as he had imagined in his fantasy, warm and soft as velvet. Her hands skimmed his hips and flowed over his back to his shoulders leaving a path of heat trailing behind, as if he wasn't hot enough already. She seemed to meld to him, matching his every thrust, driving him closer to the edge. Her intensified breathing nearly drove him crazy. He knew she was almost there, teetering at the edge. He greedily drove deeper into her. She was so hot. Her grip tightened on his shoulders. She moaned and called out his name as her muscles clenched around him. He drove one last time and with his release, he was sure he had died and gone to heaven.

Chapter Nineteen

Spinelli struggled to drive himself and Shannon to the mall because the fat suit he wore under his Santa costume pushed up against the steering wheel making it difficult to maneuver turns. He should have just changed into it when he got to the mall, but he figured he wouldn't have enough time. He'd spent too much time in bed with Shannon. Yet more time would have been nice. Thoughts of their afternoon delight made him grin like a kid.

His thoughts shifted to Shannon's safety. He simply didn't want her at the mall, so close to the action, so close to Loukas the Greek the mastermind behind everything. Yet he, Walker and Marsh agreed that the appearance of keeping things normal would allow for a better chance of catching a break in the case.

He and Shannon reached the Santa display to find Officer Miller in place as an elf with one of the usual elves at his side. Walker and Marsh watched and listened attentively.

Spinelli glanced at the long line of children who waited for his arrival. But on this particular night he didn't seem to mind the hours of listening to whiny kids that lay ahead of him.

As he saw to each and every child he couldn't help but notice the intense exchange taking place between Miller and Elf Tyler. He could only make out bits and pieces of their conversation from time to time through his earpiece. The background noise from the children rambling on and on about what they wanted for Christmas seemed to block out the key components of their discussion. He hoped Walker and Marsh could hear it all.

Finally, 9:00 p.m. arrived and the Santa display closed for the evening. Spinelli watched as Elf Tyler took off toward the locker room and motioned for Miller to follow. "I'll be right there," Miller yelled as Tyler stepped onto the escalator.

"Okay, but we don't have much time," Tyler yelled back.

Miller started to fill Spinelli in on what he and Tyler talked about while Spinelli had attended to the kids but Tyler interrupted as he leaned over the second floor railing and flashed an anxious glance toward them. "You have fifteen minutes. They don't like it when we're late."

"Okay, okay," Miller yelled up to Tyler, and then he looked at Spinelli. "Tyler is a nervous wreck, something more must be going down other than the card game he invited me to join."

Shannon pointed down the hall of one of the first floor exits. "While you guys work on figuring out what you're going to do I'm going to the ladies room."

"Okay," Spinelli said absently but it took all of two seconds for him to realize what she had said. "No wait." He couldn't let her go off by herself.

Spinelli looked at Miller. "You go with her while I talk with Walker and Marsh. And don't you dare let her out of your sight. Understood?"

"Yes sir."

"When you're done just head toward the locker rooms and I'll catch up to you."

Miller and Shannon headed in the direction of the restrooms and Spinelli found a quiet uninhabited corner in which to talk with Walker and Marsh on his cell and make their game plan.

Several minutes later Spinelli found himself standing by the base of the escalators by the Santa display with no Miller or Shannon in sight. He thought that maybe they went upstairs already. He stepped onto the escalator but it moved too slowly. He used his long stride to capture two steps at a time until he reached the top.

He entered the dark locker room and flipped on the lights. The room was empty. Still wired he asked Marsh and Walker if they could see

Shannon or Miller on any of the monitors. Both answered no. "I'm in route to the restrooms," Walker added.

Spinelli too headed in that direction. Walker came back on. "They're not there. Both bathrooms are empty. Shit."

Spinelli's feet moved faster and he could feel his heart rise up into his throat. "Shit what?"

A pause fell over the air.

"I'm just about there. Walker, what's going on?" Spinelli asked as he pushed his way through the ladies room door to find Walker standing there with Shannon's small handbag hanging from his pen dangling next to Miller's wire.

Every bit of air in Spinelli's lungs drained out and he fought to refill them.

"Marsh, you got anything?" Walker asked as Spinelli fought for air and imagined the worst.

"No nothing. The only thing I saw was Tyler enter the restaurant and the last thing I heard was Miller telling Shannon that he'd be right outside the bathroom door waiting for her. Everything seemed okay at that point. My eyes are fixed to the computer screens. Nothing's happening."

Chapter Twenty

"I'll wait right here," Miller said to Shannon as he leaned against the wall, inches away from the door leading into the women's restroom.

Shannon smiled and nodded then pushed her way through the doorway. She walked past the first two empty stalls and entered the third stall, the last in the row. There was no one else in the bathroom.

Through the noise of the automatic flush, Shannon heard the bathroom door open and the sound of footsteps. She didn't think much of it until a muffled groan echoed within the bathroom walls. Fear instantly penetrated her body; she didn't know why.

She reached up and gripped the top left wall of the toilet stall and pulled herself up as she stepped onto the toilet seat. She peeked over the top of the stall to find one of Loukas' men standing near the row of sinks. He held Miller by his upper arm. Miller's hair was dampened with sweat and his cheeks were flushed. Duct tape covered his mouth.

Turning her head, she found another one of Loukas' goons walking past the front of the bathroom stalls. She tried to scream but her throat closed, allowing no sound to escape.

The man entered the stall next to hers and she jumped down off the toilet. She reached into her handbag and retrieved her cell phone but before she could dial Spinelli the goon reached over the top of the stall, grabbed her by her hair, and pulled. As he yanked her upward, she plunged her hand into her purse and rummaged for anything that could help her out of the immediate situation. Her fingers wrapped around her glass nail file. She gripped it tightly in her hand and pulled it out of her purse. She reached back and then flung her arm forward and sank the nail file into the goons forearm. He released his grip from her hair and she dropped to the floor.

Shannon sprang to her feet and used her frantic fumbling fingers to unlatch the lock on the stall door then she threw the door open. She'd wanted to make a run for it but the goon was too quick. He wrapped his strong large hand around her tiny bicep and tugged her to a halt. His other hand held a handgun pointed in her direction, only inches from her face. Her heart beat wildly as she eyed the gun and the glass nail file still stuck in his arm. Blood dripped from the file. Oh, how she wished for Spinelli! He would know what to do and he would take care of her.

The sound of shuffling feet drew Shannon's attention, as well as the attention of her captor. They looked in Miller's direction. With his mouth taped shut and hands tied behind his back, Miller still made an attempt to free himself from his goon.

Shannon shifted her attention back to the bloody nail file and in one swift movement she reached over, gripped the file in her hand, and shoved it further into the goon's arm. He dropped his gun and released his grip on her. The gun fell to the floor and she lunged for it. She circled her fingers around the grip of the gun but before she could lift her arm, the room went dark.

Damp, musty air stung Shannon's lungs and she fought to open her eyes. She couldn't. The back of her head throbbed and her neck ached. Muffled voices echoed in her head but she couldn't make out the words. Among the voices, the distinct sound of a low tone groan found its way to her ear. She fought to open her eyes again. Her persistence paid off and she found herself staring down at her lap. Her chin tucked to her chest. She struggled to lift her head but the slightest movement caused the throbbing in her head to beat harder and faster. She shifted her eyes to find Miller sitting in a chair beside her. No, not sitting, bound. Not good.

* * * *

Marsh stared at the computer screens. "Still nothing happening," Marsh reported again over the air to Spinelli and Walker as they sprinted toward the restaurant. "Damn it. This fucking fat suit. Why didn't I take it off," Spinelli muttered under his breath as he trailed behind Walker. They posted behind a pillar and studied the restaurant, finding it hard to see through the tinted windows and closed metal gate.

"Marsh, anything on the video?" Spinelli asked.

"No, still no activity."

"What about in the parking ramp?"

"Only a few parked cars, no one in sight," Marsh replied.

"I don't get it. If there's no one left in the restaurant and all the exits are covered by cameras, why isn't Marsh seeing anything?" Walker asked Spinelli.

"The head of security," Spinelli whispered.

"What?"

"The head of security is in on it. I bet he's working for Loukas the Greek. Think about it. He's the only one who knows that we've been monitoring the mall cameras. What if he shut one off? If Marsh had access to all of the exit cameras he would have seen something, right?"

"We're on our way, Marsh. In the meantime call up the camera that shows the exit just beyond the bathroom Shannon used, and go back to your last visual on Shannon and Miller."

Spinelli could hear Marsh rapidly clicking keys on his keyboard. The clicking stopped. "I got it, the last visual. There doesn't seem to be anything unusual."

Spinelli and Walker climbed into the van. They all stared at the computer screen in silence.

Spinelli watched as the computer monitor focused on the bodies of Shannon and Miller. The last visual of them was of their backsides as they headed down the hallway corridor leading to the restroom and one of the mall exits. Just short of the restrooms was the last he saw of them on the monitor.

"Hmm, back it up again, to the point where they walk past the photo machine," Walker instructed Marsh.

Spinelli turned toward him. "Did you see something?"

"Stop, right there." Walker leaned forward and pointed at the monitor. "Look, right here. If you look past them, you can see the exits beyond the restrooms. Now start it again."

Marsh hit the forward button.

"Watch the camera angle as they get closer to the restrooms. Stop right there," Walker instructed as he leaned forward again and pointed at the monitor. "Look, the camera angle dropped, and you can no longer see the exits. As they walked toward the bathrooms someone adjusted the angle of the camera downward so Shannon and Miller dropped out of sight before they got to the bathrooms."

"Shit, I can't believe I didn't notice that," Marsh said in disbelief.

Walker shook his head. "You were probably focused on a different camera at the time. I guess we better pay the security guards a visit."

Chapter Twenty-One

Spinelli and Walker headed toward the main security office of the mall and Marsh stayed in the van.

"Anything going on?" Spinelli asked.

"My eyes are glued to the computer monitors and other than you and Walker there's no other activity taking place."

Spinelli knocked on the door to the security office. No one answered. He tried the handle but it wouldn't budge. His chest constricted, nearly cutting off the blood flow to his heart.

He pulled his cell phone from the pocket of his Santa suit and dialed the number to the mall security office. Through the doorway, he could hear a phone ringing but no one answered.

Spinelli glanced at Walker. "Step back."

Spinelli used his heel to kick the door open. The door to the small vacant cluttered office flung open. He took a seat on the high-backed office chair and wheeled himself up to the desk. He opened the desk drawers looking for any information that could possibly lead them to Shannon and Miller. Finding nothing of use, he slammed a desk drawer shut and pushed himself away from the desk. The chair rolled over a thin throw rug making a hollow echo sound. Walker glanced down then gripped the back of Spinelli's chair and wheeled it off the rug.

He sprang from the chair, picked up the throw rug, and tossed it aside. He studied the flooring, which looked normal and intact. Walker knelt down and rapped on the floor with his knuckle and again the sound seemed to echo. Spinelli glanced around the small office taking in every detail he could process. Things seemed in order.

A draft of cold air swept over Spinelli. "Walker, did you feel that?"

"Feel what?" Walker asked as he stepped toward Spinelli. "Wait, I feel it now. Where's it coming from?"

Spinelli held up his hand as if trying to determine the direction in which the draft blew. "Over there," he said as he pointed to the small sized closet door in the corner of the office.

Spinelli opened the closet door to find a couple of mall security uniforms hanging from the rod in a dry-cleaning bag. The cold draft caused the plastic bag to flutter. He reached in and slid the uniforms to the side exposing a door on the backside of the closet. He opened the door. The doorway led to a dark narrow staircase leading downward. "Walker, look at this."

Walker poked his head through the closet door and looked down the stairwell into the darkness, "What the hell? Where does that go and why is there such a cold draft? We're on the first floor of the interior of the mall."

Marsh still sat in the van listening to the whole ordeal. "What? What are you guys seeing?"

"There's a closet in the security office and the backside of the closet is actually a doorway to a stairwell leading downward," Spinelli replied. "Call up the blueprints of the mall and see what's supposed to be underground."

Marsh opened the blueprint file and viewed it on his computer screen.

"Well?" Spinelli asked impatiently.

"I'm looking. There's nothing, there's nothing underground on the blueprints," Marsh replied. "I guess this explains why I didn't see anything. They obviously took Miller and Shannon out via the underground."

"Marsh, we're going in. Keep your eyes peeled to those cameras and let us know if there's any activity," Spinelli barked.

They each grabbed a flashlight from the metal shelving unit, which stood next to the closet door. Spinelli edged his way through the closet door and the stairwell door first. Walker followed. Spinelli barely fit through the narrow stairwell. He'd been so preoccupied with everything he forgot he still wore the Santa outfit, fat suit and all. Earlier he'd shed the hat and beard and left it in the van but foolishly, he still wore the suit.

The thick cool damp air stung Spinelli's lungs as he descended the staircase. It smelled musty, like rotting wood. When he reached the bottom, he placed the palm of his hand on the cold perspiring cement wall to balance himself as he leaned around the corner to eye what lie ahead. A dim light glowed at the end of the tunnel. The ceiling, riddled with pipes running along the weak looking support beams glistened with moisture.

Spinelli and Walker headed in the direction of the light, their guns drawn, their eyes peeled, and their ears tuned in. Other than the sounds of water droplets falling from the ceiling and splattering against the cement floor, and pools of water sloshing at his feet he heard no other noises.

The tunnel turned left and the light grew brighter. The sound of vehicles passing overhead surfaced. The walls of the tunnel shook slightly with each vehicle that passed. Eventually the vehicle noise grew faint.

"We must be under the abandoned warehouse across the street from the back entrance of the mall," Spinelli whispered as he pressed onward down the narrow tunnel.

With each step they took, the tunnel grew brighter, warmer, and dryer. Eventually the tunnel dumped them into a small empty room with cement walls and a large metal door with a sliding peephole viewer about the size of Spinelli's hand. The door appeared to be locked, bolted from the other side.

Spinelli and Walker pressed their ears against the door. The sounds of at least two different muffled voices and the distinct sound of a low tone moan escaped through the doorway. Spinelli dropped to his knees and pressed his cheek to the cold cement floor. Peeking through the narrow crack under the door, he hoped to get a view of whom and what lie beyond the closed door.

Metal shelving units lined the far wall of the dimly lit room except for the gap, which a metal door occupied. Small packages that held a white substance bound in clear plastic wrap filled the shelves.

Spinelli lifted his head and looked at Walker, who met his gaze. He mouthed, "drugs," before returning to the crack under the door. He heard the snick of knuckles hitting flesh followed by a groan and a loud raspy gasp for air. Spinelli tried to see what was happening from his position on the floor but it was difficult to make out. He could identify two sets of legs, toes pointed in the direction of the gasps for air, both subjects clothed in black jeans and black boots. He recognized them as the same style Loukas the Greek's musclemen wore. Roughly, two feet in front of the musclemen he could see two more sets of legs bound by duct tape to the front legs of pale yellow wooden chairs. One set were covered by green leggings with matching green shoes that curled up at the toes, with the other set covered in nude colored nylons and small black shoes with a big gold buckle.

Spinelli froze. His worst nightmare had come true; Shannon sat beyond the door.

He willed himself to breathe. *Snap out of it…think…think.* He pulled himself up off the floor.

"What's going on?" Walker asked.

Spinelli and Walker stepped back into the tunnel and Spinelli got Walker and Marsh up to speed on what he saw under the door. They quickly formulated their plan. While Spinelli and Walker found their way through the tunnel Marsh had called for backup and two uniformed officers now stood by his side. They decided that Marsh and the officers would sneak into the abandoned warehouse and try to find the entrance to the underground room. This way they could penetrate the room from both entrances with more presence and hopefully rescue Shannon and Miller without any more harm coming to them.

It seemed like an eternity, the waiting game. It about killed Spinelli to leave Shannon in the hands of Loukas the Greek's goons until Marsh and the officers could get into place. He and Walker listened to the sound of muffled voices beyond the door while they waited.

"Marsh, where the hell are you?" Spinelli asked.

"We got a little problem up here in the warehouse."

"What kind of problem?"

"Well, it's wired with cameras up here. And though it's pitch black, for all I know they're watching us right now and we're having trouble finding the gateway to the underground," Marsh replied.

Suddenly Spinelli heard a loud screeching noise of metal being scraped across a cement floor. It sounded from the room in which Shannon and Miller sat in captivity. Spinelli dropped to his knees, and pressed his cheek against the floor and peered under the door. He saw Loukas the Greek and one of his large musclemen dressed in black enter the room through the door located between the shelving units which housed the drugs. A light glowed behind them.

Spinelli fought for a voice. "Marsh, get a move on. Loukas and another goon just entered the room. There's a light shining from where they came. Look for the glow and you should find the entrance."

Spinelli watched as Loukas glanced in the direction of Shannon and Miller then toward the goons. His voice echoed throughout the room and made its way under the door and into Spinelli's ear. "I told you to tie up the loose ends. We can't afford any more mistakes like the kid lying in the hospital. Get rid of these two now and make them disappear. And hurry up because we've got company upstairs to take care of as well."

* * * *

Tears burned in Shannon's eyes. Did she really just hear her death sentence? A multitude of visions and thoughts bombarded her mind causing her to grow dizzy, or perhaps it was her throbbing head that caused the havoc. At this point, she didn't know.

A vivid picture of her nephews surfaced in her mind. She wondered if she would ever see them again. She thought of all the things her untimely death would prevent her from doing. She would never have the opportunity to marry and have a family of her own. She wondered who would take care of Mrs. Finch and Mrs. Night. And Spinelli, who would take care of him? He needed taking care of, he probably didn't know it, but he did. Would she ever get to see him and feel the warmth of his arms around her again?

Shannon gave herself a mental head slap. *I had the gun in my hands. What the hell happened? How did I end up here?*

She blew out a sigh. *Where is Spinelli? If only he were here this wouldn't be happening, he'd know what to do, and he'd take care of us.*

* * * *

With no good plan in mind, Spinelli sprang to his feet and pounded on the metal door. He knew he needed to create some sort of distraction to buy time until Marsh and the officers could make their way down.

"Shit!" Walker cursed over the air. "Marsh, watch out; they know you're up there and hurry up. Loukas the Greek just entered the room and ordered that Shannon and Miller be killed."

As Spinelli banged on the door, both he and Walker stepped to the sides hoping they wouldn't be seen through the large sliding peephole. The peephole gate slid open for a moment, and then shut. "I don't see anyone." The muffled voice came from the opposite side of the door.

Spinelli pounded on the door again and the peephole opened.

Gunshots fired, echoing a floor above. Loukas the Greek's voice penetrated throughout the underground, "Damn it! You idiots! Can't you do anything right? Get rid of whoever it is."

Marsh's hurried voice came over the air. "We're on our way down. We're just about there."

The metal door between Spinelli and Walker pushed open and a large bodied man dressed in all black stepped through. He turned his head and eyed Spinelli standing there in his Santa suit. He appeared completely dumfounded at the sight. Walker stepped out from the opposite side of the door and tasered the goon. He dropped like a rock.

"Let her go! There's no way out for you, let her go!" Marsh's voice bounded from the other side of the room.

Spinelli stepped into the doorway to find Loukas the Greek with his arm wrapped around Shannon's waist. He was using her as a shield. Spinelli's heart popped into his throat and cut off his oxygen supply.

One of the goons stood to Loukas' right, pointing his gun in Spinelli and Walker's direction. Positioned between the goon and Shannon, Loukas stood secure.

Spinelli studied the room, looking for anything, anything at all, to help them out of this situation safely. Other than the drug-stocked shelves lining the walls, only a few old rickety wooden chairs and a table occupied the center of the room. One bare light bulb hung above the table dimly lighting the room.

Spinelli shifted his glance in the direction of the muscleman who cowered behind Miller. Miller still sat slumped over and motionless and bound to his chair with duct tape. The muscleman kneeling behind him drew his gun and pointed at the doorway in which Marsh and one uniformed officer stood.

All at once, Miller let out a loud groan and flung his head back catching the thug behind him square in the face. The crunching sound of the goon's nose bones breaking sent a shiver up Spinelli's spine. The goon immediately threw his free hand over his profusely bleeding nose. Then he pulled his hand back and stared at the pool of blood in his palm. His eyes widened as if he'd just seen a ghost. The color drained from his face, his eyes rolled back and he dropped to the floor. Out cold, Spinelli thought. But for how long?

The excitement drew the attention of the thug standing next to Loukas. Spinelli seized the opportunity and fired a round at the goon standing between him, and Loukas and Shannon. He caught him in the shoulder of his gun-arm causing him to drop his weapon and fall to his knees. Blood seeped out of his shoulder and soaked into his shirt.

Spinelli's eyes fixed on Loukas and with his gun pointed in that direction he edged toward Loukas and Shannon. He scanned him, looking for weapon. He saw none. Loukas continued to use Shannon as a shield. Spinelli watched as Marsh moved in toward Loukas from the opposite side.

Walker moved in toward the thug that lay on the floor next to Miller. He appeared motionless but suddenly, in one fluid movement, he reached for his weapon that lay only inches from his hand and quickly fired off a round at Spinelli catching him in his midsection.

In the very next instant Walker got off a shot and the thug that shot Spinelli lay permanently motionless on the cold cement floor.

All eyes shifted to Spinelli.

When the bullet struck him, Spinelli felt an odd sensation pass by his abdomen. The impact caused him to shift slightly to the left. He looked down at the right side of his body and noticed a black rimmed hole in the red velvet coat he wore. Confusion filled him. He couldn't feel pain yet he knew he'd been hit.

Shannon let out a cry and Spinelli caught her frantic gaze. She looked as confused as he felt.

Spinelli took a couple of more steps toward the goon he shot in the shoulder and he kicked the goon's weapon out of his reach. He looked up and saw that Marsh and the uniformed officer had freed Shannon from Loukas the Greek's hold and secured him.

Spinelli glanced at the uniformed officer and pointed to the thug on the floor. "Cuff him."

Walker radioed for an ambulance for Miller and cut the duct tape loose, freeing Miller from the chair.

Spinelli could hear Walker talking to Miller. "Is he okay?" Spinelli yelled over to Walker.

"He's conscious, but a bit out of it."

Spinelli took a moment to study the room then deemed the situation secure. Suddenly Spinelli remembered he'd been hit. He looked down at where the bullet entered him. No blood and no pain. He eyed the bullet hole and studied the black ring left behind on the red velvet material. He unfastened the big gold buckle on the wide black belt, which secured his coat and then he unbuttoned the black buttons and pulled the coat open to find that the bullet entered and wedged itself in the gut roll of his fat suit.

Spinelli let out a hearty laugh and looked up to find the eyes of Shannon, Walker, Marsh, and Loukas on him. "Well, Merry Christmas to me."

Shannon leaped forward, threw her arms around Spinelli's neck, and clung to him. Her voice shook, "Oh my God! I thought you'd been shot." He wrapped his arms around her and held her tight as she sobbed into the crook of his neck.

"Shh, Sweetheart, everything's okay."

Chapter Twenty-Two

Spinelli strode into Captain Jackson's office and took a seat in the chair across from her desk rather than on her two-drawer file cabinet where he usually took up residence.

"Well, what's the scoop on Loukas the Greek?" Jackson asked.

Spinelli cleared his throat. "He had quite the drug trafficking operation going on right out of his restaurant in the mall with the help of an extensive underground tunnel system reaching as far as the campus. He preyed on college kids who worked at the mall to handle the distribution."

Jackson cocked her head to the side. "What do you mean? How did he get them to work for him?"

"He would invite the kids to join in an after-hours card game in his restaurant. The drugs, alcohol, and women made it appealing to the kids. And when his card sharks would take the kids for all they were worth their options were either to cough up the cash to pay off their gambling debt or work off their debt by distributing drugs for Loukas. Most of the kids didn't have any money so they were forced to distribute. If they didn't comply, Loukas' goons would help them come to terms with their destiny."

Jackson raised an eyebrow. "Hmm."

Spinelli pressed on. "Anyhow, at some point victim Reed apparently confided in victim Hudson about the operation and they both wound up dead. The kid in the hospital, Jarrod, got pounded by Loukas' musclemen because they caught him talking to Miller. They'd discovered Miller's a cop. As it turns out, Loukas has been running this operation for twenty plus years out of the mall, recruiting new college kids in as others left the operation."

"So one minute these kids are partying and having the time of their lives and the next minute they find themselves deep in debt and desperate. Desperate enough to risk going to jail for drug distribution."

Spinelli nodded. "That about sums it up."

Spinelli lifted himself from his chair and headed toward the doorway.

She called after him and he glanced back at her. She looked unusually puzzled.

"Ah, Spinelli, why are you still dressing like Santa? You've solved the case, your undercover job as Santa is over."

Before he could answer Jackson, the sound of women's heels clicking on the old hardwood floor echoed throughout the precinct. They both turned their heads in that direction to find Shannon crossing the precinct floor dressed in her little Santa helper outfit.

Spinelli turned his head back in Jackson's direction. He flashed his lady-killer smile, wiggled his eyebrows a couple of times and finished off with a little wink. "That's why," he said as he pointed in Shannon's direction.

Jackson returned Spinelli's sly smile with one of her own. "Lord help her!"

About the Author

Valerie Clarizio lives in beautiful Door County Wisconsin with her husband and extremely spoiled cat. She loves to read, write, and spend time at her cabin in the Upper Peninsula of Michigan. She's lived her life surrounded by men, three brothers, a husband, and a male Siamese cat who required his own instruction manual. Keeping up with all the men in her life has turned her into a successful hunter and fisherwoman. She holds a Master of Business Administration degree and works as a Finance Director. She is a member of Romance Writers of America and the Wisconsin Romance Writers of America.

Twitter:@VClarizio
http://www.facebook.com/val.clarizio
http://valclarizio.wordpress.com/